Elements & a Key

Jillian Beane

Jillian Beane LLC

ISBN: 979-8-9900217-5-4 (Paperback)

ISBN: 979-8-9900-217-4-7 (eBook)

Library of Congress Control Number: 2025903817

Book Cover by Shawnna Sue

Paperback Wrap by Jillian Beane

Editing by Dayna Hart at Hart to Heart Edits

1st edition 2025

Published By Jillian Beane LLC

Contents

Prologue

Nowhere near ready to wake, Suleima was left with no choice. Gage pulled her closer with a growl. She patted his forearm where it crossed over her stomach. "Dyna and Agron are here. I need to go and see what is going on."

He grumbled, but let her up, getting up and preparing to meet their friends alongside her.

A few minutes later, as they stepped off the porch, Dynasira said, "We have news."

"What's going on?" Gage asked.

"Hamanad was able to find some information, maybe on the location of the key. His apprentice brought the information to the jinn early yesterday," Agron began, "But his apprentice arrived alone."

"Where is Hamanad, then?" Suleima asked.

Dynasira glanced at Agron before turning back to Suleima, "We don't know. "The apprentice's mind has been altered, and he has no recollection of what took place."

"Then how do we know the information about the key has not been tampered with or forged?" Suleima asked.

Dynasira handed her a metal tube. It vibrated in her hand. When the cylinder in the end popped out, pouring smoke into the air, she nearly dropped it. Within the smoke, Hamanad's face appeared.

"Suleima, if you are receiving this from anyone but me, know I have done everything in my power to keep this secure. Beyond Mount Lucent, and past the valley below, there is a swampland filled with harpies. They can be dangerous, but they value magic above all else. I have bartered with a few and been directed to head into the cave system that runs beneath the next ridge. The only entrance is through a canyon on the far side.

"If I cannot continue recording my journey, you have heard my last steps. The Fae are a people of great complexity. Like everyone else, some are truly evil, while others have hearts of gold like yours, yet most fall somewhere in the middle. Treat them as you would anyone else, and in the end, their true colors will show through. Luck to you, my friend."

Suleima looked up at the four council members standing in front of her; Kaly had joined them halfway through Hamanad's message. "Hamanad is missing."

"When do we leave?" Kaly asked.

"Soon."

Chapter 1

Since learning of Hamanad's disappearance, Suleima and her friends buzzed from place to place, gathering supplies they would need for their next journey. Unlike the trek up Mount Lucient, when it was only her and Gage, an entire envoy would accompany her to find Hamanad and the key. If Solisa, the Sun Goddess of the fae, managed to get the key first, she could unlock a spell book containing spells that would devastate naturals – people without magic—and supernaturals alike.

Gage prepared Wade to take the Alpha position with the remaining pack members at Amber Mountain, while he, Kaly, and Ryan, the pack's medic, would accompany the group. The group, which would be made up of the dragons, wolves, jinn, and Suleima, a shaman, would meet at the pack house the next day before heading off, following Hamanad's steps past Mt Lucient, into the swamplands and beyond.

Suleima sat on the edge of the bed in her cabin, packing up the last of the clothes for the trip. Movement out of the corner of her eye caught her attention. She turned her head to see the tiny, woven vine creature dancing in an imaginary breeze. She smiled and stood, walking over to the table where a shallow box of soil sat. The green fae, whom she called Koa, swayed back and forth, his movements intensifying in excitement as she approached. Suleima picked up the small watering can nearby and moistened the dirt.

The fae scrambled over to the damp spot and bent, his arm and leg vines burrowing into the soil, sucking up the water greedily.

"You are going to behave for Wade while I am away, right?" Suleima asked the miniature creature when he had his fill of the water.

The mischievous glint in Koa's eye was the only answer she was expecting. She'd found the creature a day ago, growing in the field where the Green Knight's execution took place. In that short time, Suleima learned the creature did not like being left alone. She and Gage brought it back with them and placed it on the soil bed she prepared when the two of them left the cabin to spend a few stolen moments together out in nature before their next foray into danger and the unknown. Returning, they found soil hurled everywhere, and small items around her house lay strewn about. After taking the time to clean up, she left the fae alone again, while she walked Gage to his truck, only to return to the same mess.

Suleima finished packing, grabbing the supplies she would need to perform the Ritual of Alucenia to recharge her shamanistic power, and placed them carefully into her pack along with the food stores she would need to carry. She set her pack next to the door and added her bow and arrows to the pile. She carefully bent her wrist, which had been broken a few days before, but was already healing, thanks to a benefit from her mating bond with Gage, though still sore and weaker than usual.

She gave her home one last look to make sure she hadn't missed anything, hauled her pack onto her back, slung the bow over her shoulder, and lifted the shallow box of soil with Koa safely tucked in the center. She hiked the half mile through the forest to her truck, loaded her pack into the bed, and climbed in, setting Koa on the seat next to her.

The drive down the mountain to the pack house didn't take long. Before she knew it, she was parking at the edge of the driveway. Cars and trucks filled the space between her old truck and the house—the entire pack must have come to send them off. Gage was at her door, opening it an instant after she shut the truck off.

Taking her hand, he guided her out of the cab and wrapped her in his arms. He smelled of woods and warmth.

She closed her eyes, wanting to block out the danger looming in front of them; the danger which refused to give them a moment of peace since she stumbled across the pack's path in the woods what felt like years ago, but in reality had only been a few months. Suleima pulled away slightly, looking into his eyes, taking in the violet that surrounded the natural blue-gray of his eyes since their mating.

"Are you all set?" he asked.

"As ready as I will ever be. I'm ready for all of this to be done."

"We're just going on another hike in the woods."

She laughed and dropped a quick kiss to his lips. "Yep, only a walk in the forest, enjoying nature once again."

Suleima reached into the cab of her truck and pulled out Koa and his bed of soil. Walking next to Gage, she carried it into the pack house, setting it on the table in front of the large bay window. Koa was sleeping and barely shifted, only moving when she set the shallow pan down, rolling to a sunnier spot. She smiled down at the fae creature, then walked to the next room, where Wade, Kaly, Ryan, and the other werewolves gathered.

"Thank you, Wade, for keeping an eye on Koa while we are away."

He nodded in acknowledgment before stepping back and allowing Gage to take centerstage.

"Wade will be acting as Alpha while I am gone. We'll be able to communicate through Kaly, if necessary. Stay alert. We hope it will be quiet here, while we're gone, but I want everyone watching, just in case."

Heads nodded all around the room. Gage took Suleima by the hand and led her back onto the porch as Dynasira and Agron landed in the front yard, shifting back into their human forms.

Dynasira's blue hair shimmered in the bright sunlight as she approached with Hamanad's apprentice, Tiamaned, on her heels. "Another jinn will meet us at the trailhead of the swamplands."

Suleima nodded. "We'll take two trucks as far as we can. Dyna, you and Agron can fly ahead and meet us there. Once we meet up with the other jinn, I have a feeling hiking will be our best method of following and finding clues to both the key and Hamanad."

"Agreed," Agron said.

"I am sorry I cannot be of more help finding Sir Hamanad," Tiamaned repeated for the hundredth time since he came to deliver Hamanad's message.

Suleima laid an assuring hand on his shoulder. "You got the message to us. That is the most important part, Tiam. We will find him."

Tiamaned dipped his head in thanks, his dark hair falling over his eyes with the movement, then stepped back.

"It's nearing mid-morning," Gage said, grabbing his pack from Wade. "We should head out now. It will be a long couple of days drive before we get to the swamplands."

"As much as I am loath to ride in one of those contraptions yet again," Dynasira began, "I'm sure it will be smart to conserve our energy since we have no idea what awaits us once we start hiking."

With a wave out the window, the group drove off, heading northeast, toward the mountain range of Mount Lucient and beyond.

Chapter 2

THEY DROVE UNTIL DUSK before finding a spot to pull over and set up camp for the night. After gathering firewood and helping to unload the trucks for the evening, Dynasira and Agron shifted, and curled up on opposite sides of the camp, taking point to guard for the night.

Gage was busy setting up their tent while Suleima cleared an area and started the fire.

Gage cleared his throat, interrupting the silence they'd worked in. "Uh, Sul?"

She straightened up from where she bent over the budding campfire and looked in his direction.

"We had a stowaway." He held up his hand toward her.

Koa perched on the back of his hand. He squeaked as she put her hands on her hips and shook her head.

"We've come too far to turn around now," Suleima said. "Little imp. You were supposed to stay home with Wade and stay safe."

He squeaked back again, protest evident in his tone.

Suleima shook her head and turned to Kaly. "Let Wade know where he is, please."

Kaly's eyes stared off into the distance for a moment, then cocked her head, listening for the reply. "He's been worried since they discovered Koa missing. While he's very happy to know where Koa is, the pack has already torn the house apart searching for him and will not be happy about having to clean up the mess they made while doing it."

Suleima took Koa from Gage so he could finish with the tent. She set him down away from the activity of camp, so he wouldn't get stepped on—and so he would be within eyesight while she finished with the campfire.

Quickly, Koa burrowed his vines into the ground, soaking up water and nutrients, likely thirsty after going most of the day without water and soil.

They gathered around the campfire when the tents were set up and sat in silence, each consumed with their own thoughts of the dangers they would face in the coming days.

Kaly was the first to speak. "How much longer will we be driving?"

"We're about a day from the base of Mount Lucent. It's probably another day's drive to reach the valley beyond. I hope to continue in the trucks until we reach the swampland. My best guess is two more days in the car before we have to hike," Suleima answered.

The group lapsed back into silence as Koa scrambled on Suleima's lap, giving a big yawn, snuggling in, and falling asleep.

One by one, they climbed into their tents for the night, leaving Suleima, Gage, and Koa sitting by the fire.

Speaking quietly to not wake up the sleeping fae, Suleima said, "The quiet of the forest tonight is unsettling, like the calm before the storm."

Gage squeezed the hand he was holding. "There're a lot of predators with us this time around. Two dragons and three werewolves will make the animals in the area keep their distance."

Suleima dropped her head onto his shoulder and yawned. "I guess. I'm feeling uneasy. Maybe since we're closer to Mount Lucent. Not all the memories from that trip are happy ones."

Gage placed a kiss on the top of her head. "It all worked out in the end. Come on. Let's go get some sleep."

As he helped her gently to her feet, she cradled Koa in her free hand. He only stirred a bit, before snuggling in again. Suleima pulled gently with her fire, dragging the heat and flame from the campfire, then bubbled some water out of the ground to dampen the coals. At Gage's prompting, she climbed into their tent, drifting off to sleep as soon as her head hit the bedroll and Gage's heat settled in next to her.

Stretching as she woke, Suleima immediately noticed Gage missing from the tent. Koa was stirring as well and she lifted him, placing him in the dirt outside the tent as she emerged, so he could get some water and nutrients from the soil.

Tiamaned appeared at the front of his tent, followed closely by Kaly at hers.

Sitting to the left of the campfire from the night before were three rabbits and two squirrels. Suleima coaxed the fire back as Kaly cleaned the morning's rewards.

"Gage will be back soon. He is waiting for Ryan to shift," Kaly said absently. "They had to go a fair distance to find much to hunt for breakfast."

Dynasira and Agron shifted and joined them at the fire, helping Kaly clean the game, while Tiamaned and Suleima grabbed berries from bushes nearby to supplement their breakfast, fortifying them for another long day in the trucks.

They reached the base of Mount Lucent before dusk. This time, the wolves shifted and went out hunting for dinner, while the dragons helped Suleima and Tiamaned set up camp.

The evening passed much the same as the last, except Gage and Kaly took first shift keeping guard. Agron and Ryan would take over halfway through the night, giving Dynasira a chance to rest.

This close to Mount Lucent, Suleima's alarms rang each time Gage's wolf stepped out of sight, remembering each time the tests targeted him, and she was forced to endure. Her anxiety must have bled through their bond because he would pace back into her line of sight, eyes connecting with hers across the campsite, and he stayed close until her anxiety lessened.

Dynasira stopped trying to engage her in conversation, instead chatting with Tiamaned and Ryan until they trudged off to their tents.

Dynasira waved her hand in front of Suleima's face, "Hello? What's going on in that head of yours?"

Suleima reached out with her senses, finding Gage just beyond her eyesight, and sighed. "He was in danger when we were here last. So much." She shook her head in a vain effort to shake off her worry. "I can't seem to relax."

"He probably feels the same fear for you. In his eyes, you were in the most danger and even injured by him."

"It wasn't his fault!" Suleima sharply defended.

Dynasira raised her hands in surrender. "You see it as your fault. Why would he be different?"

Suleima took in Dynasira's words, weighing them, and feeling how right they were.

"Go talk to him. I'll keep Koa out of trouble."

"Ha! Good luck with that!" Suleima said, standing and walking into the woods where she felt Gage.

By the time she made it to his side, Gage stood in human form. He took her hands and drew her into his embrace, holding her tightly.

"I do believe you and I are both shouldering the blame for things we had no control over the last time we were here," she said, snuggling into his warmth. "And we are amplifying each other's fear."

His hand dropped to her left forearm, "Dirrin didn't cause all of these scars."

Lifting her left hand to his cheek, she pulled his head so their eyes met. "The phoenix and Dirrin are the only ones to blame for these scars. And we aren't going up that mountain. We are only driving by. Let's agree to stop worrying about what happened up there. I think we have enough in front of us to worry about."

"Easier said than done, Sul."

She reached up, linking her hands behind his neck, drawing his lips down to hers. "Each day is a new day. Let's live for tomorrow, not relive the trauma of the past. I'll try my best to do the same."

He nodded, dropping another kiss to her lips and one to her nose, then stepped back and shifted, trotting off into the distance soon after, back to his patrol.

Suleima walked back to camp and gave Dynasira a hug of thanks, then gathered Koa and headed off into her tent. Before Ryan relieved Gage for the rest of the night's watch, she lay awake, keenly aware of where he was until he returned in the early morning hours. As soon as his familiar warmth filled the tent, she finally fell into a peaceful sleep.

Chapter 3

Halfway through the third day, the crude road through the valley abruptly stopped, and the edge of the swampland came into view. Suleima pulled her truck to the edge of a small copse of trees and climbed out.

"We'll leave the trucks here," she said, pulling her pack from the bed of the truck and slinging it over her shoulders. Her bow was next, then she laid a hand out for Koa, setting him on her shoulder. "We should find the other jinn soon, right Tiamaned?"

"Faramad said he would meet us at the edge of the swamps," he responded.

"Do you remember anything about being here before with Hamanad?" Suleima asked.

A cloud passed over Tiamaned's eyes before he shook his head.

Suleima laid a hand on his forearm and gave it a reassuring squeeze.

"Is there another energy vamp running around?" Dynasira asked, "Or something else that could have tampered with his memory?"

"We need to be ready for the possibility that Solisa created more than one energy vampire. But, it's possible Kylin made it out here and back in less than a day, and messed with his thoughts before we fought her last time."

Kaly and Ryan shifted to their wolves, while everyone loaded their gear onto their backs. With Gage able to shift almost as quickly as the dragons now, he planned to stay in human form for the start of the trip.

The clean, crisp air of the valley morphed into a cloying mire of humidity and rotting vegetation. The soppy earth sucked at their feet with each step. Thick vines hung from the trees; moss and fungus growing from every surface. Colossal insects buzzed close, slipping away when swatted at, only to return a moment later. Sunlight struggled to break through the dense canopy above and the foggy mist floating all around them.

Suleima opened her senses, pulling in the locations of her friends, who were getting harder to see through the impermeable fog. She could feel a few snakes, slithering away from them, turtles and frogs holding still and keeping quiet, hiding from the danger they sensed. Sizable birds fled their hunts, taking to the air to avoid the predators below. Floating just on the edge of her senses, Suleima discovered several harpies. She whistled to get the group's attention and stopped walking as they gathered close.

"There are several harpies in the area to the east."

"Should we go to them before we find the other jinn?" Dynasira asked.

"They are already here," Tiamaned replied.

Every head spun in his direction, and Suleima stepped back at the sudden appearance of two jinn she never sensed nearby. Gage's growl rumbled over the chirps and bird call cacophony floating over the air.

Kaly's silent snarl was plainly visible where she stood at Gage's feet, echoing his anger.

Tiamaned backed away from the group, his hands up in surrender, while one of the other jinn stepped forward. His hair was dark like Hamanad's and he had similar features, a chiseled profile, and a strong chin.

He dipped his chin in her direction before speaking. "You must be Suleima. I have heard many stories about you from my father. I regret that this is our first meeting. My father kept me busy at home and abroad to keep me from the fights against Dirrin. With his disappearance, he can no longer keep me out of this. I am Faramad."

Suleima's brows rose in surprise, but she recovered quickly, reaching out a hand to shake his strong one. "Hamanad spoke of you when we first met. The way he spoke of you, I thought you were much younger. It is nice to finally meet you, though I wish it was under other circumstances."

"He often treats me as if I am still a child, so I am not surprised he speaks of me in the same way."

Agron looked past the jinns who appeared so suddenly as if searching the fog for more to appear. "How did you appear without any of us sensing you?"

"Ahh, that would be the talent of my friend, Nadiram," he said, indicating the young woman standing behind him, a willowy woman with long, loose hair and vivid green eyes, though one eye was clouded and likely blind.

Nadiram stepped forward and held out her hand to shake Suleima's. A sudden loss of her connections to the elements, took Suleima's breath.

The instant aggression buzzing across her bond with Gage had her reaching out her other hand to touch his arm, staying his movements as she tugged her hand away from Nadiram.

"Apologies," Nadiram said, releasing Suleima's hand.

Suleima pulled with air, clearing the fog away from their group, making it easier to see everyone. Gage's anger still blazed through their connection as he covered her hand with his, which still rested on his arm.

"My talents lie in the disruption of magic, rather than as a healer. I've not learned complete control of my abilities yet."

Suliema flexed her fingers and shook her hand, trying to shake off the horrible, echoing feeling from when she lost her magic on Mount Lucent.

"We thought Faramad would be alone," Tiamaned said, shaking Nadiram's hand. Nadiram's magic did not appear to affect him.

Faramad cocked his head at Nadiram. "She managed to cloak herself until we were too far to turn back." He continued murmuring, "Can't control it when we want her to though."

"I hear you," Nadiram responded, shoving past him. "Hamanad protected and cared for me since my parents died when I was small. I am not about to sit home and wait for word from *you* when I could be out here *doing* something."

Gage spoke up, distracting the jinn from their rising tensions. "There are harpies to the east. We were about to head that way."

"Not those harpies," Faramad countered. "Those are just guardians. They won't have the information we need, though they would happily take your payment before telling you they have no information. Follow me." He turned on his heel and headed west.

Suleima stepped in line behind Faramad. The others gathered behind, picking their way through the swampy mess at their feet.

Reaching an area wide enough to stand shoulder to shoulder, Suleima stepped up next to Faramad, "What sort of payment are they going to be expecting?"

He glanced down at her, then turned back to the complicated path they were following. "These harpies value magic above all else. They will require bartering with magical spells or artifacts. Or they will force you to show your magic through some kind of challenge. Since we know my father came through here, I am hopeful they will give us the information they already gave to him."

"That's unlikely," Gage chimed in.

Faramad nodded absently. "Yes. If we want to find him quickly, we will doubtless need a great show of strength."

Suleima took in the information as she scanned the area looking for more harpies in the direction they were headed, keeping quiet as she scanned the area. She found them a moment later. She reached an arm out, stopping Faramad's progress and halting everyone behind her. "There is a group of seven harpies heading this way." She pushed with air, fanning the mist away. In the distance, the silhouettes of the harpies barely registered. Their giant wingspans flapped in the air as they coasted over the ground.

The closer they got, the more details revealed themselves. The harpies had immense talons at the base of each leg. Their bodies, covered by feathers, were shaped like a woman's. The frontmost harpy's feathers shifted colors, a pearlescent sheen to them, her long dark hair reaching down to her talons. The harpies behind her had hair colors spanning the rainbow in various lengths.

The harpies stopped and hovered in the air about ten yards from where her group stood. Sharply hooked beaks present on each of their faces revealed the potential dangers the harpies posed. They keyed into the werewolves, glancing at one another, then back to the wolves.

Quiet clacks and taps of their beaks were interrupted by a sharp caw from the harpy in the rear with short, purple hair. The sounds of the swampland abruptly halted with her call.

Lowering his eyes and bending his head slightly, he spoke. "I am Faramad, son of Hamanad. We come looking for information to find my father."

The redheaded harpy snapped her beak violently in their direction, followed closely by the harpy with swampy green hair.

Faramad stepped back at the implied threat, but Suleima held her ground. "Hamanad sent word that he came through this area. He was heading for a cave system. We only need directions to the canyon entrance."

The group of harpies drifted apart, closing in around the group, flanking them on all sides.

"Get ready," Faramad said, adjusting his stance. "Defense and aiming to stop them, *not* kill them."

Gage shifted, and his snarl reverberated through the swampland. The harpies were too close for Dynasira and Agron to shift without stepping on one of their group.

Suleima shoved outward with air. Caught off guard, the redheaded harpy flipped end over end. A blue-haired harpy dodged by flying above, but it left enough room for Agron to step forward and shift, leaping into the air. The deep green of his scales was camouflaged by the mossy canopy above them, making him all but disappear despite his enormous size.

One minute, Dynasira and Nadiram were behind Suleima, the next they were gone from sight and Suleima's senses. At her friend's disappearance, Suleima fought her rising panic.

Gage paused in the midst of harrying the green-haired harpy, who used the distraction to wrap her talons around Gage's neck and the base of his tail, lifting him from the ground.

Gathering her power, panic threatening to overwhelm her, Suleima pulled water up from around her feet. Pushing with her whole body, adding air to shape the water and give extra force, Suleima sent waves out in all directions.

They took the legs out from under the two jinn still in their circle and must have broken Nadiram's concentration because she became visible a moment after Dynasira took to the sky a few yards outside of the harpies' circle. The waves reached the harpies' shoulders, tumbling them through the air.

Gage took advantage and swiped his front paw at the harpy holding him captive, catching her leg and opening a gash. He dropped to the ground and snarled his displeasure.

Two of the harpies spun away from their group, but Dynasira's spray of water blocked their path before Agron landed, his bulk blocking those harpies as well as another, while Dynasira hovered above to prevent them from flying away.

Suleima pulled at air again, pushing the harpies behind her. Kaly and Ryan each snapped at their talons and tails, pushing them back to the group of harpies already trapped. Raising her bow, Suleima readied an arrow to fly as the last of the harpies were enclosed by their group. Their positions reversed from where they started.

Koa peeked out of the collar of Suleima's jacket where he'd been sleeping and shook his fist at the rounded-up harpies.

When the harpies didn't move, Suleima lowered her bow and approached the one Gage injured. She reached out her hand slowly, carefully watching the harpy for any sudden movements. Beyond lightly clacking her beak, the harpy stayed still. Suleima pushed a bit of pain relief into the harpy's leg. Faramad stepped forward, and Suleima moved aside so he had access to heal the injury with his magic.

Inside, Suleima beamed with pride at the way they'd teamed up and worked together, despite not having fought alongside them before. Hamanad taught his students well. A bittersweet pang pulled at her heart and tears gathered in her eyes. She would find him, no matter what, or how long, it took.

Chapter 4

With the green-haired harpy's injury healed, the harpy with the red hair approached, clacking her beak quickly at Faramad.

He turned to Suleima. "They are inviting us into their den, and will provide the information we seek."

Suleima furrowed her brow in confusion but nodded and motioned for Dynasira and Agron to stand down. They shifted and gathered back into the group, while Gage, Kaly, and Ryan stayed in wolf form, remaining on the edges of the group as guards. It took Suleima a moment to realize that her continued unease came through her bond with Gage. She maneuvered her way to the edge of their group to lay her hand on the scruff of his neck.

He glanced at her for only a second, resuming his constant scanning of the area around them. She projected a feeling of calm to him. This time, he looked at her sharply before stepping out of reach.

Message received, Suleima curled her fingers against her hand, missing the touch of his fur, and stepped back into the center of the group. No one spoke as they picked their way through the marsh until they reached the mouth of a cave barely discernable from the rocky outcropping surrounding it.

The redheaded harpy led the way in, while the others stood with their backs against the cliff face. Faramad followed the harpy, Suleima on his heels. Still unsure of their safety, Suleima held her magic at the ready, keeping a wary eye on the harpy.

The harpy turned abruptly, snapping her beak at Suleima and Faramad. "She's asking us to sit," Faramad translated.

Suleima cautiously pulled out the chair—carved from a single log—and sat across the table from Faramad, who did the same. Tiamaned stood at the entrance to the room, watching.

The air in the room shifted with the slow undulation of the harpy's wings, keeping her aloft.

Silence reigned for several minutes before the harpy clacked her beak.

"Hamanad, another jinn, came through here about a week ago. We are trying to find him. Can you tell us the direction you sent him?" Suleima said.

Rapid chirping and clacking answered her.

"She says my father marched through the swamp, headed for a canyon on the far side of the next ridge."

More rapid clicking and tweeting followed by a whistle was obviously directed at Tiamaned.

"She wonders why Tiamaned did not give us the directions, as he heard them the first time."

Tiamaned's head dropped in shame. Suleima stood, walking over and placing her hand on his shoulder. "He cannot recall the details. Someone altered his memories." She faced the harpy once more. "Have you seen any fae through here recently?"

The harpy flew backward a pace and clacked her beak violently.

"They do not welcome the fae here," Faramad said. "She says there was a disturbance at their borders the day after Hamanad passed through their lands, and again a day after, but the guardian harpies never saw who it was. They moved too fast."

Suleima closed her eyes and sighed. "Thank you."

A single clack echoed through the room in response.

Suleima prepared to leave, only to be clacked at again.

"We are to find a different route when we leave. She says we will not be welcomed back into the swamplands once we pass through," Tiamaned translated.

"Understood." Suleima motioned for the jinn to precede her out of the room. "Thank you again."

Exiting the cave, Suleima gathered her group back together and walked in the direction indicated, leaving the rainbow-colored harpies behind them. The presence of the guardian harpies on the edges of the swamplands, Suleima kept close tabs with her magic to make sure they stayed a safe distance away.

About a half-hour into their march through to the other side, Suleima finally spoke. "When we reach the edge of the swamplands, we'll climb up and over the next ridge. There's supposed to be a cave entrance on the far side of the canyon. It's the last we know of Hamanad's steps. The journey through the swamps will take us at least a full day, so keep your eyes peeled for a good place to set up camp later."

"At least we will only have one night to sleep here," Dynasira said, picking up her mud-covered shoes, a look of disgust plainly visible on her face.

Faramad helped her build their fire. She used her power over water to push the groundwater away from the area and dry up some of the nearby fallen vegetation to burn.

They worked silently in tandem for a while, but once the fire gave off a cheerful crackle, Suleima spoke. "Your father has played an important role in my life, particularly since Erist's death. He's there for guidance at a moment's notice. You have my word that I will not rest until he is found and reunited with you."

Faramad dipped his head in acknowledgment, a small smile playing across his features. "He would return with epic stories of the battles you fought together. I may have sat, enraptured at his knee, just like the child he portrayed me as." His tone became solemn. "I believe he spared me most of the losses your side endured. But, I could see the haunting in his eyes when he returned from the first battle you fought against Dirrin."

Her nod of agreement ended with her chin on her chest and her eyes brimming with unshed tears. Suleima's eyes closed as a wave of sorrow threatened to overwhelm her. "We lost so many that day." Hamanad made it out of that battle unscathed, but the losses would haunt her for the rest of her days.

Jonah.

The name echoed through her mind as memories flooded in.

The Setura pack had left her floundering when she asked them for help. But Jonah and the other rogue werewolves stepped up. Jonah had taught her how to fight, and how to protect herself and others, without magic. The skills she learned with him were invaluable. They helped her save her life and the lives of many others time and again.

The visual of the fatal blow he took on the battlefield that day crystalized, unbidden, and tears spilled silently over her lashes.

Quiet reigned over the camp. Her somber mood seemed to blanket the whole of their party.

Gage and Kaly took up the first watch. He'd kept his distance from her since she tried to calm him.

Suleima searched for their bond, but it felt muted, closed off to her. She robotically shuffled through her usual camp activities, helping to set up the tents and gather berries to supplement their dinner, puzzling over Gage's reaction. Koa didn't stray far from her, crawling into her hand, absently patting it with one of his tentacle-like vines, as if he felt her melancholy.

She'd barely touched her dinner when she cleaned up and excused herself for the night. Dynasira promised to douse the fire later.

Rather than lay in his makeshift pan of soil, Koa curled up next to her head, patting her head, until he dozed himself.

Suleima stared up at the ceiling of the tent, waiting for Gage to return, falling into a fitful sleep long after the rest of the camp bedded down for the night.

Gage climbed in and lay beside her, not touching her, well after he should have returned from his watch.

She couldn't stop the tears sliding silently down her face at his distance. A moment later, she felt the bond open, and Gage's quick intake of breath before he gathered her close. Suleima rolled to face him, burying her face in his chest, soaking up the warmth and comfort his presence always brought her.

With the bond blazing between them, she could feel his fear and uncertainty, but she didn't try to calm him again. A loud sob was all that emerged when she opened her mouth to speak.

Gage tightened his hold on her and dropped a kiss on her hair. He spoke quietly. "I know you meant well, trying to calm me. But here, with everything happening, I need to be alert. The attention of the guardian harpies on us—something about it was wrong. I can't explain it."

Suleima leaned away to look into his eyes, searching the bond to find his unease. She dropped her forehead to his chin and pulled in a steadying breath. "I'm sorry." Clasping his hand, she continued, "I trust your judgment. I didn't notice anything, but we can't dismiss anything right now."

Now that she found it, his unease was apparent, and he still didn't relax.

"Who's on guard now?"

"Faramad and Agron. Where are you going?" he asked, sitting up.

Suleima placed her hand in the center of his chest. "You need to rest. You won't rest well with just Agron and Faramad on watch." She ignored his protests and took up a post not far from their tent.

Chapter 5

Suleima noticed the harpies just at the edge of the reach of her senses. She chose a spot to keep watch and concentrated on the large group. The harpies hovered on the periphery, unmoving. She assumed they were there to usher her group out of their territory without dawdling. Several large predatory birds flew overhead, giving the area around her group a wide berth. They also veered off at an area on the edge, near the harpies, but not with them. There was an odd sense of something flirting with the periphery of her senses—never quite coming close enough to discern what it was. When it would've been close to the harpies, they all retreated beyond the scope of her senses.

Brow furrowed, Suleima stood and took a step.

"No one would be happy to see you leaving camp alone. Most especially the Alpha not resting in your tent." Dynasira's disembodied voice came from behind her.

Suleima spun to face her—having been so preoccupied with the harpies and the unknown entity that she didn't notice Dynasira's approach. "You should be sleeping."

"As should you."

"I've not taken watch yet. It's my turn."

"You've not been given watch because no one, especially Gage, wants you out here alone."

"I'm not helpless. I'm as much a part of this team as you or him."

Dynasira laid her hand on Suleima's shoulder. "No one says you are helpless. We want to protect you. There is no telling what we will run into out here. You've been the key to our success so far. You being rested and ready is our first line of defense."

Suleima squinted her eyes, ignoring Dynasira's comment, gazing out into the darkness. Her eyesight was no better than the average human, so they told her nothing as her magical senses brought back the same creature, a predator, flirting with the edge of her reach.

"What do you see?"

"I can't *see* anything. But something is out there."

"The harpy guardians were out there earlier."

"They still are, but something else is near them."

Dynasira took a step in front of her. "Go back to the tent."

"No."

"Sul..." Gage's growl came from behind her.

"You don't want me to calm you. I get it. I won't." She spun to face him. "But you will *not* keep me wrapped in a bubble for the rest of my life either. I am as capable as the rest of you. I've proven it time and again, have I not?"

"It's not about your abilities..."

She spun away, cutting him off mid-sentence. "I asked you to keep an eye on Koa. I don't want to return to a torn-up tent." Suleima stomped out into the darkness, not waiting for a response. She didn't close down the information flowing through their bond—she wouldn't do that to him.

Suleima picked her way through the marsh as best she could in the dark, tripping occasionally on a mossy tree root in her path. The guardian harpies kept their post, but whatever was with them backed away as she walked, keeping out of her range. As she came upon them, they clicked and snapped their beaks at her, gesturing with their wings back toward the camp.

"Who is out here with you?" she asked.

More furious snapping and pointing back to camp was their only response. She waited while Faramad caught up, sensing him following her since she walked off.

"They are instructing you to return to the tents," Faramad translated.

"I got that much," Suleima deadpanned. "Who else is out in this area?" She placed her hands on her hips and waited.

The frontmost harpy clacked her beak at the one bringing up their rear, who then spun and floated off into the distance.

"We should return..."

She glared at him, and he stopped speaking. "I'm not leaving without answers."

The harpy returned a few minutes later and chirped at the group.

"They say the creature is an ally."

"The 'creature' is staying just out of my reach, but it's been watching us for a while. I want to know why."

Faramad glanced at her in surprise. "Someone is watching our camp?"

More squawking and feather ruffling.

"They say the creature means no offense."

"Then it need not watch us." Her tone brooked no argument: it was an order. "If it continues to watch us without making itself known, it will no longer be considered an ally, but a threat. Make sure the creature is aware of this."

Without waiting for Faramad, Suleima turned on her heel and headed back the way she had come.

Gage was the first to exit the tents, as dawn broke. He quietly approached and sat with her, close but not touching.

Koa scrambled off his shoulder and into Suleima's lap where he curled up and sighed contentedly.

He pulled absently at a nearby clump of grass, the wind blowing away the shredded pieces. "I'm only trying to protect you, Sul," he blurted.

"I protected myself long before you were around. I am not helpless."

He blew out a sigh of frustration. "I never said you were helpless."

"Then stop making me feel like it." Mindful of Koa, she stood and walked away. She put Koa down near the campfire, bubbling some water up from the ground for him, before heading into her tent to pack up.

She let the fae fabric she found at Erist's glide through her fingertips. She didn't know why she packed it, only that she couldn't leave it behind.

She was zipping up her bag when she felt that creature again, at the periphery. She dropped the bag to the floor and rushed from the tent. This time, the creature didn't stop. Suleima grabbed her bow.

"Dyna!" Suleima ran across the small clearing they'd used for their camp. She instructed Agron to keep an eye on Koa, and without waiting for Dynasira to catch up, took off into the cover of the trees.

Suleima pulled up a shield around herself, reinforcing it with her fae water magic. She held offensive magic at the ready when Dynasira caught up with her.

"What is it?" she asked.

"The presence from last night. An ally, according to the harpies. He's close enough for me to sense. It should be impossible, but I need you with me to be sure."

"Stop here," Dynasira ordered. "Let him come to us." In the next breath, her enormous blue dragon took up every available space. Her tail wrapped in front of Suleima as another shield.

A few minutes later, a man ambled into view. His face was covered with a long scraggly beard that did nothing to hide the vicious scar running from his hairline across his face, disappearing under the thick unkept beard. A pronounced limp replaced his usual easy gait, and his left arm hung at a strange angle as if he couldn't fully extend it. He looked so different, she wouldn't have been able to identify him, except for those familiar neon-green eyes.

"Jonah?" Suleima's voice was barely a whisper as she lowered her bow.

Chapter 6

He gave the slightest nod.

"How?"

"You'll have to speak louder. My hearing is not as good as it was."

"How are you here? I thought—after the cyclops—how did you survive that hit, and that fall?"

Dynasira shifted and approached them, shock and awe on her face. "I was so focused on getting Suleima healed that I left the clean-up to the other dragon clans after that battle. They told me there were no survivors among the werewolves."

"I am so glad to see you. I've never been able to properly thank you for the training you gave me. It's been invaluable and saved my life and others so many times." Suleima closed the distance between them, lightly touching his hand.

Jonah flinched from the contact, and Suleima dropped her arm.

"Come back to our camp with us?"

He shook his head slightly. "You have wolves with you."

"They are no threat to you."

"Just join us for a meal," Dynasira added quickly when he looked about to refuse again.

They headed back to camp, only to find the way blocked by Gage and his wolves.

Suleima could feel the rage pumping through their bond and stepped between Gage and Jonah. Her eyes never left his as she spoke to Dynasira. "Take Jonah to the fire and get him something to eat. I'll be right behind you." When Kaly stepped into the path, at what was likely an order from Gage, Suleima pulled up a shield, herding Kaly back to her spot at Gage's shoulder.

She waited until Jonah was safely seated beside Dynasira in camp before speaking. "Jonah poses no danger to you or your pack." Her voice was lethally calm. "Do not for one second think I will allow any aggression toward him. If you can't be nice, keep your distance. He is a rogue wolf. He doesn't want to lead your pack. He doesn't want to *be in* your pack."

Kaly looked sharply at Gage before taking Ryan by the shirt sleeve and pulling him deeper into the woods, away from camp.

"Who is he? And why is he here?"

Suleima took a calming breath. "That is Jonah. I told you about him. He's the wolf who taught me to fight without using magic."

"You said he was dead."

"I thought he was. He was hit by a lethal blow from a cyclops the first time I faced Dirrin. I don't know how he survived it."

"Necromancy? Who's controlling him?"

"There's no necromancy. He's alive. No one is controlling him. As for how he is here— I can't find out more information about him, while I stand here arguing with you. So, how about you tone down your Alpha and let me speak to my friend."

Gage blew out a frustrated breath, but a growl still reverberated through his throat belying his simmering anger.

Suleima placed her hand on Gage's forearm, giving it a slight squeeze. "I'm guessing here," she began, "But your frustration with me, and mine with you, over the last few days is bouncing back and forth over our bond. Our bond is intensifying our feelings. We need to sit down and talk."

"Let's talk now."

"Not now," she replied, shaking her head. "I need to go and talk to Jonah, and you know it." She stepped into him, pulling his forehead down to touch hers. "You have nothing to fear from him." She dropped a kiss to the end of his nose. "Go for a run with Kaly and Ryan. We will talk after."

"No."

She raised her eyebrows at his tone.

He took a deep breath. "I can't leave you right now. I don't know him. He's a strange wolf."

"He won't hurt me."

"That has nothing to do with it."

She searched his eyes, then nodded. "You can come too, but I need you to promise me you will not show aggression to him. He's my friend."

Gage growled viciously.

"It's no different than when I speak to Dyna or Agron."

Gage didn't reply, just took her hand and led her back to the campsite, his body language announcing his territory like a beacon.

Suppressing her frustration to calm the emotions grating over their bond like sandpaper, Suleima let him lead the way back. She dropped his hand to bend down, picking up Koa, before sitting on the log beside him.

Gage's arm went immediately around her waist, pulling her closer, his other arm crossing to rest on her thigh. When she tried to get a little space, he only tightened his grip.

Suleima ignored his behavior and focused on Jonah. "What happened? How are you here?"

Jonah looked around at the people buzzing around the campsite.

"They are safe to speak around," Suleima assured him. "They're all allies."

"I don't have any recollection of being hit by the cyclops. I remember waking up in a bramble bush. I don't know how long I was even in there. Everything hurt. A thunderbird was there, lifted me out of the bush, and flew me away. I woke up days later in a thunderbird compound not far from here. They helped to heal me as best they could. Most of the injuries were too severe for even my accelerated healing to overcome." He paused a moment, looking around again. He seemed to weigh a decision, then clamped his mouth shut and remained quiet.

"Have you stayed here since you healed?" Dynasira asked, drawing his attention back to her, which had been locked on Gage.

Suleima covered Gage's hand with hers as she heard the low rumble of his growl but kept her attention on Jonah.

Jonah's voice became quieter. His chin dropped to the side, showing he was no threat. "I lived in the thunderbird compound nearby for months. Knowing I was the last of the rogue wolves who stood with you, there was no reason for me to return to the lands outside of Setura. When I was healthy enough to protect myself, I found a new area to settle in. The harpies and I have come to an agreement. We largely leave each other alone, but I am allowed to pass through the swamplands, and we warn each other of possible dangers. They let me know when Hamanad passed through here and alerted me of your larger group when you appeared."

"You've seen Hamanad?" she asked.

"No. I was only told of him passing through."

Suleima's shoulders dropped a bit.

"But, I know the route he took. I can lead you there if you want." Jonah's head tilted and his chin dropped further, as if preparing for rejection or scolding from an Alpha.

Suleima spoke up before Gage could. "Please. We would be very grateful for any help."

"You will be out of the swamplands by the end of the day if we leave soon."

"We plan to leave as soon as the camp is packed up," Dynasira answered.

Suleima turned to Gage. "Have Kaly and Ryan come back to help tear down the camp, so we can be on our way soon." Dislodging herself from his iron grasp, she stood and carried Koa over to where Jonah remained and sat, pointedly ignoring Gage's growl. "How are you, truly?"

Jonah glanced at Gage who glared from across the fire and kept silent.

Suleima dropped Koa on the ground and stood, walking over to Gage and pulling him to the edge of camp. "I want to speak to my friend. I need to speak to him. Go find Kaly and Ryan."

"They are already returning," he answered, tapping his temple.

"Then go find something to do that isn't staring daggers at Jonah," she huffed. "Now." She spun on her heel, dismissing him, and walked over to retake her place beside Jonah near the fire.

"He's protective of you," Jonah observed absently. "Very."

"He's my mate."

"And this friend?" he asked, indicating Koa clumsily chasing after a leaf blowing on the ground.

"He's a long story, which I can tell you about during our walk out of the swamplands. For now, I want to know how you are."

Jonah's head lowered again. "I survived."

"We both did. But, not without consequences." Suleima dropped her glamor, holding her hand out to him, twisting it to show the mottled, scarred skin.

Jonah gaped at her.

"These are why I never knew you survived. I was practically dead myself when Dyna pulled me off the battlefield that day. It was days before I was awake for longer than a few minutes at a time. Weeks before I could even move. Had I known you were alive..."

"As you saw earlier, I don't hear as well anymore. My skull—they told me it was crushed in on one side. Whether from the cyclops's club or the landing, I don't know, but it damaged something permanently and I don't hear well on the right side." His voice was hushed as he spoke. Low enough she didn't think the shifters working around them could hear. "My shoulder and hip were both shattered. The thunderbirds told me the bone fragments had obliterated the muscles, tendons, and ligaments. While my range of motion is improving over time, it may never be what it once was. I move well enough to not slow your group down if you want me to escort you along the path Hamanad took."

"I'm not worried about you slowing us down, Jonah. I am just glad to see you." Suleima gently patted his knee and stood up. Jonah lifted his hand, placing it on her forearm, and she heard Gage growl.

Jonah flinched at the sound and lowered his hand before speaking. "Your bow?" He nodded at the weapon she'd rested against a log near the fire.

"Gage has added on to the training you started."

Jonah's quick "Good," was punctuated with a nod.

Chapter 7

THEY TRAVELED IN SILENCE while they hiked through the remainder of the swampland. Suleima busied herself, surveying the area with her senses for anything out of the ordinary. Gage brooded, keeping Suleima close, putting himself between her and Jonah at every opportunity. Suleima rolled her eyes and tried to ignore the behavior as much as possible. Koa bounced from one shoulder to the next, taking in the scenery as they walked. His chittering was one of the few things that broke through the sounds of the animals of the swamplands in the distance.

It was dusk by the time the group cleared the edge of the swamplands. Between one step and the next, the ground went from spongey to dense and there was an abrupt stop of foliage delineating the border. Pinks and oranges blazed across the sky as the sun dipped lower.

Suleima held up her hand stopping the group's progress and scanned the open area stretching in front of them. Beyond a few insects and birds flying above no other wildlife occupied the open meadow.

Jonah stepped up beside her, and she turned to face him, ignoring Gage's growl.

"If we get to the other side of this clearing, there is a small outcropping of rocks and some trees nearby which can be used for cover for camp tonight."

Suleima nodded, following the direction Jonah pointed.

"This could be a trap," Gage grumbled in her ear.

"I trust him. *You* should trust *me*." She sped up, increasing the distance between them, but she still felt his irritation through their bond.

It wasn't long before they reached the spot Jonah indicated, and the group dispersed, setting up camp. Suleima grabbed Gage by the arm and tugged him out of sight and hearing of the others, rounding on him the moment she stopped.

"What is wrong with you right now?" she asked incredulously.

"What's wrong with me?" His frustration was on full display. "How can you ask that?"

"I'm asking because you are acting like an...." She stopped herself before she made things worse. Suleima took a calming breath and stepped forward, taking his hands, her thumbs absently running over the back of them in lazy circles. She pulled him to a nearby tree and sat, tugging him down to join her. She encouraged him to take a few calming breaths with her, taking in the serenity of the quiet surrounding them. Her voice was calm when she spoke this time. "What has you so upset?"

"Where do I begin? The harpies, you trying to calm me when I needed to be alert, the sudden appearance of a dead wolf from your past, the unknowns of this whole journey."

Suleima took a moment before responding. "Let's take one thing at a time. You said the harpies were giving you a bad feeling. I wonder if they paid more attention to you, Kaly, and Ryan because of their agreement with Jonah. It would make sense if they watched you more carefully because of the potential danger you pose to him."

Gage listened, nodding in agreement, before Suleima moved to the next topic.

"We already talked about what my calming does to you, and I won't do it again. Jonah's appearance, as I said before, isn't a threat to you *at all*. He doesn't want to be pack; he doesn't want to be an alpha; he doesn't want me." She heard his low growl even as she spoke and dropped her forehead to his. "You are my mate. I'm not going anywhere. I don't *want* to go anywhere. I knew Jonah before I met you. Had there been any interest there on either of our parts, we could have done something about it then. You have *nothing* to be jealous of." She crawled into his lap, entwining their fingers and snuggling as close as possible. She soaked in his strength, breathing in his scent. "As for the unknowns and dangers ahead, we have proven to be stronger together on more than one occasion now. It isn't just you and me, like on Mount Lucent. We have our friends with us. The dangers may be getting tougher, but so are we."

Gage tipped her chin, their lips meeting in a kiss that melted away any residual anger between them. When he pulled away, he kissed the end of her nose. "I think you are right, the bond is echoing our emotions back and forth, making things a bit more volatile. I don't like it. He's a strange wolf. I don't know him. He'll need to prove himself to earn my trust. But I trust you."

"Please don't shut me out again."

"I won't."

Suleima and Gage returned to a fully set up camp. Kaly and Ryan were busy preparing dinner while Dynasira and Tiamaned were stationed at the perimeter, keeping watch. Jonah sat quietly just outside the light of the fire, watching the interactions and listening to the stories Agron and Faramad were telling, trying to one-up each other. He declined her invitation to join them by the fire, insisting he was happier watching from afar.

"Once a rogue, always a rogue," he assured her. "Too many people around make me nervous, more so now."

She made sure his plate was full before heading back to the fire, to sit beside Gage. Since their conversation, their bond had calmed. No longer grating like sandpaper and inflamed with negative emotions, it floated, buoyed by contentment and love. She leaned into him, snuggling into his warmth, and watched the fire dance. The flames licked at the logs, crackling and sending sparks to float lazily back down, some settling on the stones used to create the makeshift pit and winking out a moment later.

They could barely see a sliver of the moon through the branches of the trees helping to hide their presence.

In the calm, her eyes drifted shut and she snuggled in closer as Gage's arm tightened around her.

The sensation of falling jolted her awake as Gage stood abruptly. "The harpies are at the edge of the swampland, clacking their beaks loudly. I don't know what it means," he said. His frustration and worry bled through their bond.

Agron rolled to his feet, ran to the edge of the clearing, and shifted. He tilted his head and then started clicking his jaw in the rhythm of the harpies.

Jonah stood watching him closely. His brow furrowed before he turned to Suleima. "I can't hear them and the dragon while trying, I think, to repeat the clacking, it makes no sense. I need to get closer to hear."

Gage's hand shot out, blocking Jonah's progress. "You don't go alone." The command in his voice was obvious and Jonah bristled.

"Safety in numbers, Jonah," Suleima chimed in swiftly. "Please." Suleima scanned the area, but nothing stood out.

She watched from the edge of camp as Gage and Jonah started into the clearing.

Everyone still within the boundaries of camp were on their feet and alert, scanning the darkness beyond. Kaly was shifting; Suleima could feel the pull of the pack's magic to hasten the change. Ryan bounced on the balls of his feet as his head swiveled from one direction to the next, never stopping for more than a second. She felt Dynasira and Tiamaned pulling in closer to camp from their positions.

A pained shout rang out from where Gage and Jonah had disappeared into the darkness. Suleima searched the bond and felt uneasiness and aggression, but no pain. Suleima pulled a shield around herself and ran into the darkness where they disappeared. She pumped her fae water into the shield, not knowing what might be out there. Pulling at the earth, she sped up, reaching Gage in seconds. She expanded the shield to encompass the three of them and checked them over as best she could with her limited night vision.

The coppery scent of blood reached her immediately, but with the dark clothes they had on, there was no way for her to tell where the injury was.

"Get back to camp!" Gage shouted, his jaws already beginning to elongate.

Suleima grabbed his arm, "I can't get Jonah back alone."

Gage growled but clutched Jonah beneath both arms and began hauling him back to camp.

"I heard them. Right before." Jonah's breathing was labored from pain, his words coming in stilted phrases. "Suleima, get out of here! It's a pauguk."

Gage spun to face her. "What the hell is a pauguk?"

"It's a kind of fae," she said, pumping more magic into her shield. "They are skeletal looking. Their skin is thin with no muscle beneath. They are bounty hunters. They fire invisible arrows, and they have very few weaknesses."

"How do I kill it?" Gage demanded.

"Separate the bones. Shattering is better, then we turn them to ash."

Back at the edge of camp, Suleima could see Jonah in the firelight. Blood ran down the skin of his right arm and there was a hole in his shirt at the top of his shoulder. Gage gently squeezed Jonah's uninjured shoulder before spinning on his heel and sprinting to the clearing. She called for Faramad and Ryan, quickly explaining about the invisible arrow, before taking off after Gage.

She found a furry Gage crouched in a patch of tall grass and hurried to him, covering him again with her shield.

"He won't be invisible, but his arrows are," she whispered. "He's a hunter, so his aim will be impeccable."

Wind picked up in the clearing, gusts pushing Suleima further to the ground.

Suleima strained against the wind, pushing to her knees as Gage growled beside her.

Lightning streaked across the sky, illuminating the hoard of harpies along the border of the swamplands.

"That wind the harpies are conjuring will throw off his aim." Suleima pointed in the direction she'd seen the pauguk in the latest lightning flash.

Kaly was emerging from camp at the pauguk's flank.

Through their bond, Suleima watched Gage slink off to flank it from the other side. "Careful!" she shouted over the wail of the wind and fought to her feet.

Dynasira tried to fly into the clearing, but the winds buffeted her away.

Suleima fought against the wind with each step she took. Pulling at earth to increase her speed wasn't working, so she rooted herself in place and pulled at the earth beneath the pauguk. Slowly working at it, she pulled him inch by inch closer to her, so Gage and Kaly would flank him from angles nearer his back, outside of his peripheral vision. The glowing red orbs of his eyes blazed as he fought against the earth binding him. He worked his bow, but the arrows he seemed to fire weren't hitting her.

Suleima pulled at long grasses near the pauguk, growing them longer and thicker, directing them to wind around his wrists, binding his arms in place and forcing him to drop his bow.

With the pauguk bound, the wind abruptly stopped and the lightning ceased, the last crack of it revealing the backs of the harpies as they retreated back into the swamplands.

The sounds of the others, tearing the pauguk to pieces, echoed in the stillness of the night.

Chapter 8

Suleima ran back to camp to check on Jonah. Ryan and Fara-mad worked furiously trying to staunch the flow of blood. The only part of the arrow visible on the ground next to him was the tip, covered in Jonah's blood. Suleima picked up the arrow and tossed it into the campfire. The flames sizzled and sparked around the arrow.

Jonah's shifter healing kicked in, closing the wound on his shoulder as Ryan wrapped his arm to his torso, giving time for the healing to work on the muscle and tendon damage which would take a bit longer.

"I'll take the wrap off in the morning," Ryan said. "You should be good as new by then."

A mirthless laugh was Jonah's only response.

Dynasira approached from the darkness of the clearing. "We've torn it to bits. Now what?"

Suleima sighed. "Gather the remains in the center of the clearing, far from any trees." She directed Nadiram and Tiamaned to collect firewood and bring it to the remains. Suleima picked up the end of a long log sticking out of the campfire, one end still flaming, and carried it as she followed Dynasira.

Pulling at the earth, she made bare a spot about six feet wide and laid the stick in the center. Kaly brought bones one by one in her mouth, while Gage, who shifted back to human, carried bones by the armful.

Suleima took the bone from Kaly's mouth, ignoring the icky feeling it gave her, and placed it in the center with the stick she'd pulled from the campfire. She directed Gage to leave his load in a pile at the edge of the circle for now. Sitting next to the clearing, Suleima closed her eyes and cleared her mind. Her hands trembled with the knowledge of what she needed to do. She was far from calm and reached for her bond with Gage, wrapping the comfort she felt there around her like a blanket. He hurried back with another armload, and instead of returning for more, lifted her into his lap.

His arms wrapped around her middle, caging her in and promising support and protection and the tears silently fell.

Nadiram was the first to arrive with branches and wood piled high in her arms. She dropped a few pieces into the now-dying flames from the log Suleima brought and placed the rest in a pile near the other bones before backing away to make room for Tia-maned to add his pile.

Everyone backed away slowly, giving Suleima room. She closed her eyes and pulled at fire. It came to her call, sparks popping from the dying embers and catching on the newly placed wood. A small push of air fanned those sparks into flames. She released the air she held and outstretched her unsteady left hand, the glamor dropped, exposing the scars to the night. The song of fire blazed through her middle, coaxing her deeper, threatening to overwhelm her. The pull of fire was addictive, terrifying her. Her soul wrapped around her mating bond, anchoring her further, and Gage physically tightened his arms around her.

She jerked at fire, the flames exploding and raining sparks onto the dirt. The flame's intensity increased, changing from orange and red to blue and white. The heat threatened to steal her breath. Gage shifted their positions, hauling her further from the fire.

Changing her focus slightly, Suleima pulled on air, fanning oxygen-rich air into the flames, coaxing the fire hotter. As the lone bone in the fire turned to ash, she nodded at Dynasira, who added more of the bones and wood to the inferno. The fire raged, becoming a white-hot bonfire, pushing everyone back further.

Despite the heat blasting her in the face, Suleima shivered against the chill invading her body. The fire absorbed all her concentration to keep it contained and her hands shook with the effort. She didn't notice, until Gage once again tightened his hold on her and buried his nose near the scar from his mating bite where her neck met her shoulder, that everyone else had left the area.

Without an audience, the tears fell in silence no longer. She heaved great sobs as the fire she held twisted and burned her within. She fought back her fear, her hesitation, and with Gage's strength supporting her, pulled harder and faster urging the fire's temperature higher and higher. The hotter it was, the faster the bones would turn to ash and the sooner she could let it go.

It seemed like hours passed by when she finally released her pull on fire and allowed her fae water magic to douse the flames. She turned her body into Gage and buried her face against his chest, exhausted and completely spent. Gage cradled her there, sitting in the pitch darkness of the night and the silence surrounding them. He let her just be for a long time before speaking. "I know fire scares you. But you've said before you didn't like fire before being burned by Dirrin. Why?"

She hesitated, unwilling to relive the moment. "I was maybe nine years old." Suleima fidgeted, wanting to escape the memory.

⁕⁕⁕

Erist took her by the hand, leading her out to the steel ring containing the fire. He held out his hand and she felt the power pulse as he tugged at the fire, coaxing the embers back to life. He released it moment later, and the fire faded back to embers.

"Your turn, Sul," he guided her closer to the fire, then knelt at her feet, waiting and watching the flames.

Suleima pulled with fire the way she felt Erist do it, but nothing happened. No flame rose. Not even a spark. She recentered her concentration and tugged again, only to yield the same results.

Erist turned to her. "The skill is no different than pulling on earth. Same technique, only a different element. You've learned to pull on water and air, and it is the same. Yes?"

Suleima nodded and tried again. The flames exploded into an inferno, shooting out in multiple directions. Erist dove out of the way, but not before receiving a nasty burn on his hand.

Erist pulled back on the flames, bringing them back to embers within the ring, but that was when she saw it—a kitten had ventured into their yard and received a blast from Suleima's fire.

Suleima rushed to the kitten, afraid to touch her and cause more pain. The devastation she felt at harming the innocent creature brought her to her knees at its side. She lifted her eyes to Erist. Brimming with tears and pleading for him to help, she waited for him to yell at her for the careless mistake.

Erist picked up the tiny kitten, careful not to touch the burned areas, and placed her in Suleima's reluctant hands. "Pay attention to what I am doing. We are going to start a brand-new lesson now."

Erist showed her how to ease its pain and gave her the kitten to care for.

"You know it wasn't your fault," Gage said, hugging her close.

"It still felt like it was. It was my fire. Erist *and* the innocent kitten were hurt, by me." She held up her left arm. "Maybe this is my penance. Scars to carry that mirror hers."

He pressed his finger to her lips to stop her from continuing that line of thinking. "What happened to the kitten?"

"She grew up. Her hair never completely grew back, but she survived. Caring for her, I learned what herbs worked best on burns and how to provide pain relief to anyone injured. She was a feral kitten, never really taking to being a pet, so she lived in the wild. I did catch a glimpse of her with kittens a few years later."

"That kitten helped you learn the healing you have come to use and rely on. There was no malice. It was an accident which you did your best to atone for."

"The pain, the pitiful sounds, the damage— I could never atone for that. *I* did it."

"You were young, just learning about fire. Mistakes happen. It's what comes after that counts."

Suleima gently removed herself from Gage's lap, steeling her knees from the threat of collapse at their exhaustion. "The destruction of fire is one I'll never get over." Head shaking solemnly, she stepped out of his reach and coaxed her earth magic, pulling with her small amount of reserves remaining. Suleima vibrated the dirt below the ashes, pulling them deep within the soil and sprouting up grasses, erasing the evidence of the fire.

Gage guided her back to their tent and waited while she recharged her power wells. He helped her inside and enveloped her in his arms as she settled into an exhausted sleep.

Chapter 9

SULEIMA FINGERED THE LUXURIOUS fae cloth as she packed up camp and prepared to move out for the day.

Gage stopped and watched her curiously. "Why did you bring that?" he asked.

Suleima shrugged. "I'm not sure yet." She carefully refolded the fabric and placed it in her backpack. Grabbing Koa, Suleima left the tent and approached Jonah who was staring quietly into the fire. "How are you feeling this morning?"

"No worse for wear," he replied, eyeing the fae creature sitting on Suleima's knee.

Quietly dancing to the beat of his own drum, Koa bounced from foot to foot and waved his arms around, before sliding down Suleima's leg and soaking up his breakfast from the nutrient-rich soil at their feet.

"What is the next leg of the trip?" Suleima asked.

"We need to go up and over this ridge."

Gage emerged from the tent. "Any new and exciting creatures waiting for us on this ridge?" He sat next to Jonah, covertly checking him over.

Since Jonah had tried to get her to leave the danger of the clearing with the pauguk. Gage's hostility was absent.

Jonah looked up and watched the people milling around the campsite, packing and prepping to leave before speaking. "I've heard some old jinn tribes are scattered throughout the area, but I've only encountered the harpies and natural wildlife... well, and now the pauguk."

Tiamaned spoke up. "I don't think Hamanad or I encountered any of the jinn tribes—at least, I don't remember it if we did."

"What is the first thing you do remember, Tiamaned?" Suleima asked carefully.

"The tube with the message from Hamanad was in my hand. I'd pulled it out of my backpack. I stood at the base of Mount Lucient. Then I headed straight to you."

"And the last memory before that?" Dynasira asked from behind him.

"Hamanad and I were heading to the swamplands. I wondered why we weren't skirting the edges to avoid the harpies. He said he needed to talk with them."

The path to the top of the ridge was long and winding, barely wide enough in a few places for even a single person to walk along. Every head was on a swivel, looking for any sign of danger. Suleima kept her senses open, scanning for anything that could pose a threat.

Several strange, goat-like animals with humped, broad shoulders, smushed in faces, and deep barrel chests bleated at them as they walked by. Birds with enormous wingspans flew overhead, casting shadows on their path. The trees and shade were sparse. The steady wind whistled through the tall grasses waiting to be cut short by the strange goats.

Suleima caught the smell of smoke and stopped, searching the horizon.

"I smell it too," Gage said from behind her. "Let's keep moving."

The group kept their pace, reaching the summit shortly past midday. The smoke they could now see came from the canyon. Trees hid the flames and surrounding area from sight. Before she could ask, Dynasira and Agron shifted and flew toward the smoke. The rest of them began to pick their way down the rocky path, skidding down several feet at a time in many places.

When Dynasira returned, landing carefully and shifting, she spoke rapidly, "We can't see anyone around the fire. We'll keep scouting and see you at the bottom." An instant later, she was airborne again.

Everyone was exhausted when they finally reached a plateau, still several hundred feet from the canyon floor. Dynasira and Agron joined them as they paused to rest and have some food.

"No one approached the fire, but it is still burning as if being attended." Agron's gruff voice announced his frustration.

"Has the shape of the fire changed? Like logs being added or broken down? Or is it completely unattended and being kept going by magic?" Suleima asked.

"I can't tell."

Nadiram raised her hand slowly. "I can try to approach."

"Absolutely not!" Faramad protested.

"Not alone," Suleima interrupted the argument brewing. "Dyna or Agron can take her close and stay with her to check out the fire. Anything goes wrong, get back in the air."

"We will both go," Agron chimed in. Before Dynasira could protest he added, "I'll stay out of sight once we land. But the two of you aren't going in without backup."

Plan made, the larger group kept moving while the dragons flew Nadiram toward the fire.

Reaching the bottom of the canyon floor was a welcome relief from the steep incline of the path they'd just trekked. No sign of Dynasira and Nadiram yet, though Agron still circled lazily above. The trees were packed close together, making it impossible to see into the distance. Their branches and leaves created a canopy so thick that no sunlight penetrated from above. Jonah and Gage took point, while Kaly and Ryan walked at the group's flank, their superior vision in dim lighting made it easier for them to navigate the uneven ground.

As the smell of the campfire grew stronger, Suleima stopped the group. "We've not heard anything from Dyna and Nadiram. Agron is still above. We need to be cautious." She tilted her head, listening and scanning with her senses. "Something is off. I can't sense Dyna or Nadiram."

"If Nadiram is cloaking her, you wouldn't sense them," Faramad interjected.

"True, but Agron is still lazily circling. He wouldn't still be doing that with us down here He would have landed and at the very least come to give us a report of what he has seen."

Gage shifted, and his hackles rose.

A picture developed in her mind. He wanted to leave the rest of the group here. Only the two of them would venture closer. Suleima stepped out of the group, stopped, and turned to face them. "I don't know what we are going to find. Stay here. Gage can relay to Kaly what we find. Until then, I'm going to put up a ward around all of you. I don't want anyone to be able to reach you." Suleima knelt and buried her fingers into the dirt. She used her fae magic to strengthen the ward and tie it off before standing and addressing them again. "You will be able to pass through to get out. You aren't trapped in there. But please, stay there until Kaly gives the all-clear or we call for help."

Pulling a shield up in front of herself and Gage, they headed deeper into the wooded area, the acrid scent of smoke growing stronger with each step.

Nothing appeared to her senses. Dynasira and Nadiram were nowhere to be seen, and Agron was still above, circling. The pattern was too repetitive for it to be natural. Gage's silent snarl showed his agreement with her assessment.

Suleima sent Gage a few feet to her left, where he would be well hidden by a bramble bush, and she stepped to the edge of the clearing. She let out a shrill whistle but saw no reaction from the shadow circling above. The fire merrily crackled in the center. It wasn't magic fire. She could tell from here that someone had been tending it, but they weren't in sight. Suleima called on her fae water and took another step. Closing her eyes for a moment, she pictured what she needed, opened her eyes, and released the power she held. Heavy mist drifted down from above and settled into the clearing.

For a moment, nothing looked different. Then someone moved, disturbing the mist, revealing their location. That one movement set off a chain reaction as she watched at least ten people in motion. Having a specific location to pinpoint with her senses, Suleima concentrated and found what had been hidden from her.

A group of jinn were in a surrounding camp. Dynasira, Agron, and Nadiram were clustered together at the edge. Their movement was restricted as they fought against the bindings holding them in place and hidden.

She sent Gage an image of where she felt their friends, sending him to protect them, while she took another step into the clearing further exposing herself.

"I am Suleima, a shaman from Amber Mountain, friend of Hamanad of the jinn." She projected her voice across the clearing. "My friends, the dragons and jinn you currently hold, are helping me to find Hamanad and get him to safety. We mean you no harm. We only look to aid our friend."

A disembodied voice echoed back to her from many different directions. "Hamanad is not the only reason you come."

"True," she answered. "We are also looking for a key. A special key which will open a very dangerous book. A book we do *not* want to see opened."

"Leave this place!"

"Not without my friends." Suleima's matter-of-fact response was punctuated by a howl from Gage, as he, the dragons, and Nadiram backed away from camp, heading to where they left the others. Never taking her eyes off the clearing in front of her, she felt Gage circle back and come to rest at her side. Suleima pulled with air and lifted the mist into the air high above the trees, allowing the jinn to remain hidden. "We are leaving now. Do not attempt to stop us." The command in her tone halted the movement of the jinn approaching her from the side.

Her fingers tingled and she aimed her focus on the fire in the center of the clearing. A slight push with fire and the largest log, in the center of the fire, popped loudly and split down the middle.

She backed up one step, then another, until she was back in the trees. She kept her senses locked on the jinn.

"Let's not rest anywhere near here. I'd like to steer clear of those jinn. We can hike a few more hours before we set up camp. No one was harmed, only detained. Grab something to eat from your pack along the way and we can get moving." Gage told the group as they came into view.

She nodded and picked up her pack. Her legs ached from the trek down the steep side of the ridge, but putting space between them and the jinn here was the smartest move.

Nadiram approached her about thirty minutes into their hike. "I'm sorry I couldn't keep Dyna and myself cloaked from them. I didn't realize they would have my affinity for magic."

"No need to apologize. I agreed to let you find out what was there. We always knew there was a risk you couldn't hold the cloak. I'm simply glad everyone is OK."

"They said they don't know where Hamanad is. I believe that. They were cagier when it came to questions about the key, but at least they spoke to us. Other than tying us up, they were relatively kind."

"Why did they tie you up?" Kaly asked.

"They saw through the cloak." Dynasira rubbed her wrists. "I assume they just didn't like us coming into their camp hidden."

"I think they could see me because they have the same affinity. Once I knew what to look for, I could see a shimmer where they stood, even while cloaked. I'm the only one in our jinn community who can cloak myself and others, hiding their magic. Most of our community is healers."

Agron stepped forward. "I didn't know something was wrong, or I would have flown back and warned you. I heard something and came in for a closer look. They didn't have to touch me to disrupt my magic. One minute, I was in dragon form, the next I was falling to the ground as a human, and couldn't shift back. I think they swarmed me. I felt several sets of hands, but I couldn't *see* anyone. As Dyna said, other than being tied up, we weren't mistreated, so I didn't want to escalate to violence. I knew you would find us."

Suleima nodded. Gage dropped back, letting Jonah lead them through the still-dim woods and closed his hand over hers.

"They are fine. No one was hurt. We got them out." His voice was quiet and lyrical, the gruffness usually there smoothed away.

Suleima pulled in a deep breath and tried to listen to his words, tried to take comfort in them, but she was the reason they were all out here. Her fight with Dirrin. Her fight with Kylin. Her inevitable fight with Solisa. She was the common denominator here. It was all her fault.

He stopped walking, pulling her to a stop with him. Kaly moved to the front with Jonah and kept the group moving forward. Gage pulled her in, wrapping his arms around her, and sat against a nearby tree, pulling her into his lap. His hand absently rubbed her back as he pulled her chin, looking into her eyes. "All this doesn't fall on you. Every one of us who fought beside you, every one of us out here with you right now, is out here because we believe in you. We fight alongside you because you fight for what is right. None of us want the Dirrins and Solisas of the world to rule. The Council of Erist formed to make each and every one of these conflicts matter to the greater good. It doesn't all fall on you. Don't take the weight of the world on your shoulders, Sul."

A moment of silence weighed heavily around them before he spoke again. "I want you to think about something. Amber Mountain was always going to be a battleground. But what could we have done against him, just me and my wolves? He'd have annihilated our pack. You brought us magic, dragons, jinn, and thunderbirds. Only by working together were we able to defeat him." He held her close a moment more, squeezing her one last time before helping her to her feet and standing beside her.

Suleima was lost in thought as they stood, the words he spoke tumbling around in her mind. She hadn't looked at it that way. He was right. Eventually, Dirrin would have made it to Amber Mountain, possibly stronger than he had already been by the time he reached the pack's territory. He'd hurried to Amber Mountain because he knew that was where Suleima settled. How much more power could he have amassed before coming there? And it was her magic, her journey that brought them the key pieces they needed to defeat Dirrin.

Kylin was a pawn, the same as Dirrin, sent to take out the threat Suleima posed. Would Solisa have sent her if Suleima hadn't killed Dirrin? Maybe not. But their next fight would be Solisa. She didn't know if she would have the power to take down Solisa on her own, but they were stronger together.

Chapter 10

Suleima wanted to be as far from those jinn as possible before stopping, so they hiked until full dark. Sitting around the fire before guard assignments were arranged, she spoke up. "We are still about a day's hike from the entrance to the cave system. No one is to stray from the camp tonight or tomorrow. There are too many unknowns now. We don't know where Hamanad is or how far between here and there he was taken. We don't know what shape he will be in when we find him. And the key is still a mystery to us. Solisa still wants it, that much is certain. The pauguk is enough evidence for me. She wants that book too much to stop."

Dynasira interrupted, "Have you heard from Zenisa recently? Does she have any information or insight?"

Suleima shook her head. "No. Not since she left Amber Mountain."

"Is she going to help us with Solisa?" Agron demanded.

"She said she would help. But what that 'help' means to her, I don't know."

Eventually, the conversation around the campfire grew quiet, everyone lost in their thoughts.

Koa prattled around the campsite, looking for attention from everyone who would give him any. His lighthearted antics were a welcome distraction.

Suleima felt on edge.

She walked to the edge of the furthest tent, buried her fingers in the soil, and layered a ward over the area. When she finished, she faced everyone. "No one leaves the area tonight. Stay within the wards at all times."

"Why?" Gage asked.

"Just a feeling," she answered simply.

He nodded and headed to inform the others.

A spark and pop in the campfire woke her. Suleima slipped out of Gage's arms as quietly as possible and emerged from their tent. A quick scan showed everyone in their tents—no one on watch. Suleima pushed more of her will at the ward, strengthening it, calling her fae water, and feeding it into the ward as well.

The fire continued to pop and fizz, sending sparks into the air. Suleima walked to the edge of camp laying her hand on the ward, feeling it pulse and flow around her hand. She scanned the area with her senses and sensed no one except the flaming red-haired beauty sauntering in her direction. She was tall and slim, wearing a deep red sweater and black jeans. The flames in the palms of her hands cast an eerie glow on her face. Like Zenisa, her hair blew behind her in a wind existing only for her. Her eyes danced with the flames reflecting from their dark depths. The bone structure of her face was sharper than Zenisa's but the resemblance was obvious.

The flames of the campfire roared in response to the presence of the fae on the other side of the barrier.

Suleima pulled at the fire, trying to contain it, but her efforts were futile.

A smile appeared on Solisa's face. She must have been able to feel Suleima's attempt and failure to control the fae's effect on the fire, even through the barrier of the ward.

Solisa stopped at the edge of the ward and slowly lifted her hand, extinguishing the flame covering it. She reached forward and attempted to rip the ward down as Zenisa had done after Zia died. A split second of surprise showed on her face before determination replaced it and she tried again.

"I've learned a few tricks since you sent Kylin," Suleima taunted. "You can't pull this down."

The fire roared behind her. Suleima concentrated on a new ward, one to surround and contain the fire in the ring of rocks behind her. While the flames licked at the barrier now limiting it, the fae water built into it sizzled and popped.

"Fae?" Solisa's head tilted, curiously eyeing Suleima. Her eyes narrowed at her. "An abomination. No wonder Dirrin jumped at the chance to face off against you. Even if he was unaware of your true nature, he'd have known instinctively that you were different. Kylin, too. No matter," she waved her hand dismissively, "Fae blood or no, you don't stand a chance against me."

The fire raged, pushing at the new ward, but Suleima held fast. Sweat formed from the effort it took to contain the fire and to keep Solisa from penetrating the barrier between them. She refused to acknowledge the filth spewing from Solisa's mouth.

"You won't stop me. I'll have my key." Solisa's comment was not as nonchalant as Suleima believed she was aiming for.

"How can you want to use those spells? Enslave and imprison those who would oppose you? Why?"

"Those who oppose me?" Solisa cackled. "My dear, those who oppose me will be dead. Those who bow before me will do my bidding, spared from death."

"So death or enslavement are the only options? Not much of a choice if you ask me."

"If you don't want to die, stay out of my way."

It was Suleima's turn to laugh, "Of the two options, I'd rather be dead." She turned away, dismissing Solisa.

"Dirrin and Kylin were weak. You may have defeated them, but you cannot defeat me."

"If they were so weak, why did you use them?" Suleima shot back over her shoulder. She knelt, holding out her hand for Koa, who climbed into her hand and continued climbing until he rested on her shoulder. When Suleima turned back to face Solisa, she heard the intake of breath and saw the momentary widening of her eyes. "The Green Knight was your warrior. Your prized possession. I defeated him as well. I wonder what this new version of him would think of you?"

In that moment, Koa stuck out his tongue at Solisa and Suleima laughed.

"I guess that answers that," Suleima said. "Where's Hamanad?"

"I guess you'll never know."

The fire behind her exploded through the ward she built. The force of the release shoved her to her knees. Solisa sped away, cackling.

In the blink of an eye, Gage was shifted and by her side, snarling at the edge of the ward where Solisa had stood. Dynasira, her royal blue dragon taking up a good portion of the warded area, sprayed water on the fire that had escaped the ring of rocks in the explosion.

Kaly blinked wearily. "I didn't leave my post. I wouldn't leave my post."

Suleima placed a hand on Kaly's shoulder. "It wasn't your choice—some sort of fae magic would be my guess. No one stirred in camp but me when she arrived. Agron wouldn't have left his post either. I think Koa and I were the only ones not affected. Koa, because he is fae, and she wouldn't have known about him. Me, likely because I was who she wanted to speak with."

Suleima found no trace of Solisa or any other creatures when she scanned the area.

"Does she have Hamanad somewhere? Are we even going in the right direction to find him?" Faramad asked desperately after Suleima finished recounting the visit.

"We have no leads to go on except the directions Hamanad sent in his search for the key."

Faramad stomped off in frustration and Suleima hung her head.

"I want to find him too," she whispered. Gage's hand on her back brought her comfort in the uncertainty. Was she making the right choice?

"If we don't find the key before Solisa, finding Hamanad will do us no good," Dynasira said, walking up to the group again in human form. "Faramad knows that."

Chapter 11

IN THE LIGHT OF day, the scorched grass surrounding the firepit was a sharp reminder of their visitor the night before. Suleima's fingers tingled as they passed over the embers which were barely warm—a completely new sensation.

Gage sat beside her.

He traced her forehead as she concentrated. "What's going on in there?"

She looked up at him and tried to find the words to explain. "The fire feels different to me now—the fire for the pauguk, it got so much hotter than I've ever been able to do before. And now, the embers... I feel them like I feel earth magic through the soil."

"You've been forced to use your fire magic more. Could it simply be the additional practice?"

She waved her hand over the long-extinguished coals and watched as the smoke began to rise anew. "Erist made me practice with fire. It never changed how it felt." She pulled the heat away, and the ember cooled as if the fire had never been. She shook the tingles from her hands then stood, lifting Koa into his customary spot on her shoulder, and lifted her bow.

Suleima and Gage joined the rest of the group and began the long hike for the day.

As they walked, Suleima pulled from the charcoal nestled into her bag and a spark popped in her hand, easier than she remembered. Brow furrowed, she caused another spark to pop, this one bursting above her palm and raining down like a firework.

The pull was easier; she wasn't wrong about that. But there was something else different and she couldn't put her finger on it.

She stopped trying to puzzle it out and focused on the beauty of the landscape they traveled. The lush greens and earthy browns and grays reminded her of home. They brought to her a sensation of peace even in the chaos of their journey.

A wave of comfort and contentment wafted like a breeze through her, but this one wasn't from her; it sang through her bond with Gage. Her eyes snapped up to where he walked with Ryan. He glanced back at her, and even at this distance, the rim of purple around his icy blue-gray eyes showed.

The sun beat down on them with no breeze or shade for relief. They pulled to a stop near a small copse of trees near lunchtime for a much-needed rest. In the distance, a crack of thunder sounded, vibrating the ground beneath them. Lightning struck, raising the hair on her arms and the wind suddenly kicked up, ripping leaves from trees and screaming through wildly bending branches.

Suleima struggled to stand against the wind, gripping a nearby tree trunk to keep her balance. Koa huddled into the pocket of her shirt as a chunk of hail the size of an acorn smashed into the tree right above her hand. She flinched away as a shard broke away, bouncing off the tree and slicing across her cheek.

Suleima pulled at the air, trying to counter the wind and slow it down, but as soon as she thought she had a hold of it, the wind whipped harder. A fist-sized chunk slammed into the center of her back, dropping her to her knees. She hastily pulled together a shield, expanding it to cover the group as Gage called everyone in closer.

The hail bounced off the shield, shattering and piling up around the perimeter, but the wind buffeted through, forcing them to their knees.

Struggling to keep her balance on her knees, Suleima leaned against Gage as she pulled on her senses. The gusts of wind were tossing plant and animal life alike, making it hard to pinpoint anything around them. She closed her eyes and reached for his hand to help ground herself.

It was then she spotted him. Untouched by the weather around them, a nuberu approached their shield.

The nuberu would have barely reached her hip if he'd stood next to her; only the enormous, brimmed hat pulled low on his head added to his height. Straggly wisps of hair stuck out of the hat in all directions, but his long dark beard was thick and braided. His dark brown hair and speckled leather clothing helped blend him into the surroundings.

Spotting him, Gage shifted, his snarl ripped away by the wind. His claws dug deep into the ground as the wind whipped and lashed at them, pushing them against the shield, the only thing keeping them all from tumbling ass over tea kettle through the trees.

Suleima pulled at the earth *inside* the shield and coaxed thick roots up and around the legs of each of her companions to anchor them in place. Lightning struck a nearby tree, the trunk splitting down the center, sheering off half to fall against the shield, making Suleima grunt at the effort to keep the shield intact. Gage and the other wolves, still in their human forms, howled at the deafening sound. Her ears were ringing too.

She allowed herself a quick steadying breath then jerked at fire. Flames erupted in a blast of fireworks within the trunk of the fallen tree. The concussion from the crack throbbed along the exterior of her shield, sending rippling soundwaves over the surface. The remains of the tree splintered in two and fell away, clearing her view.

The nuberu kicked up large chunks of hail as he waded closer to the shield. Wrinkles carved the dark gray skin covering his face and hands. The overly large nose hooked and curved to the side as if broken repeatedly in the same spot. Bushy brown eyebrows nearly hid his beady black eyes. But the leathery, bat-like wings protruding from his back stole her attention.

She yanked at the earth near the nuberu, narrowing her eyes and fighting against the wind. The first vine she pulled at, elongating it to grasp at the nuberu, blew in the opposite direction. She concentrated on keeping it in his line of sight while pulling on another on the opposite side of him. The manufactured wind aided her this time. The moment it was close enough, Suleima wrapped the second vine at the base of his wings and yanked, spinning and lifting the nuberu, so he hung upside down, suspended with his wings now trapped against his body.

The hail began anew, intensifying in size and amount, battering the shield and at least knee deep.

Gage's jaws clamped lightly around her arm, getting her attention. Nadiram's mouth moved furiously, but her voice was lost in the wind. Suleima squinted her eyes as Nadiram slowed her words, annunciating them carefully so Suleima could read her lips.

Closer. If Suleima could get her closer, Nadiram could interrupt his magic.

The nuberu struggled against the vine trapping him. She wound it tighter, forcing his wings to bend awkwardly. The speed of the wind increased more, stealing her breath. Her eyes watered, drying in the force of the wind, making it hard to see beyond the edge of her shield. She closed them and focused on what her magic could see. The dwarf-like creature had an odd sort of glow around him that ebbed and flowed with the intensity of the wind. She focused on it a moment.

Suleima pulled at the vine holding him, slowly dragging it closer and closer to their shield, while the nuberu screeched and fought to escape. His long, spindly fingers swung wildly at the vines, but she kept them just out of his reach.

Sweat beaded on Suleima's face as the nuberu closed in on the outside of the shield and she split her concentration. With him so close, the hail stopped, but the wind whipped relentlessly. Suleima pulled at the roots holding Nadiram in place, dragging her, inch by inch, against the wind and nearer to the edge of the shield where the nuberu hung, trapped but still fighting.

Nadiram fought to her feet and reached her hand into the air. She carefully pushed her hand through the hole in the shield Suleima created.

The glow surrounding the nuberu retreated as Nadiram's hand inched closer. The golden glow's color dulling near her hand and blazing brighter beyond.

The wind retaliated, a thick, broken branch flying through the air, bouncing off the hastily formed shield in front of Nadiram's arm.

Struggling with the final distance, Suleima pulled the nuberu an inch closer, allowing Nadiram's hand to close around his wrist. Instantly, the wind quieted, and the hail stopped altogether. Nadiram drew in great gasps of air, her brows drawn in with concentration and effort as she fought to maintain contact with the reeling nuberu.

"Can you hold him?" Suleima asked.

"Not for long," Nadiram answered, her voice strained.

Gage snarled viciously and snapped his teeth at the nuberu who squealed at an ear-piercing decibel. Those who could covered their ears with their hands against the sound. Gage's ears pinned back against his head.

Chaos erupted. The nuberu swung his arm wildly, catching Nadiram's arm with his claws, leaving deep gashes in their wake. He continued to wail as he wiggled free of the vine and took to the skies.

Dynasira and Agron were in the air a blink of an eye later, but the nurberu was long gone. Tiamaned and Faramad went to work healing Nadiram's arm, while the rest tried to gather what they could rescue from the knee-deep hail.

When everyone gathered together again, Suleima laid a ward around them.

"What the hell was that thing?" Agron asked, taking a bite of his jerky.

"A nuberu. They can control the weather," Suleima answered. "They are fae, but I could see his magic around him—a strange golden glow. His magic didn't come from within, I don't think."

"Is that common?" Dynasira asked.

Suleima shrugged at the same time Jonah spoke. "Not all fae carry their magic within." Every head swung in his direction. "The harpies are a distant fae cousin. Their magic is not contained within. They access the magic around them, like shamans. Unlike shamans though, they can pull from the magic around them at a near-limitless rate, like other fae."

Chapter 12

Suleima's muscles ached and exhaustion pulled at her as the group set off to finish traversing the path to the cave opening on the far side of the canyon floor. Gage shifted back to human form and walked with her, his arm wrapped around her to keep her steady on her feet. Several times, he tried to suggest they rest longer, probably feeling her exhaustion through their bond, but she insisted they keep moving. His frustration at her persistence bled through the bond, but she wasn't willing to add any more time to their travel than absolutely necessary.

The mouth of the cavern opened up in front of them as the sun began to set. By now, the routine was set and everyone went about setting up their camp. At Suleima's suggestion, the fire was started at the opening, and their camp set up inside. "We'll be protected by two sides if we set up here," she explained. "I'll be able to set a stronger ward in front of and behind us and our posts will be easier to patrol."

As soon as everyone was occupied, Gage approached Suleima. "Lay the wards, then recharge and sleep."

"I can help..."

"By getting rest," he interrupted. "You are nearly asleep on your feet. I feel how drained you are, how drained you have been since the encounter with the newboo."

She chuckled. "Nuberu," she corrected.

"Ugly, winged dwarf thing," he countered.

"Rest," Dynasira chimed in as she walked past, shaking her finger at Suleima under the bundle of firewood she carried. "And ugly is right." She bumped Gage with her elbow.

"Rest while you can," Jonah piped in as he carried his bedroll to the back side of the opening.

"Fine!" Suleima let out an exasperated sigh. "Everybody's ganging up on me," she pouted.

"Because you take care of everyone else first. You need to take care of yourself." Nadiram added, "I've been banished to bed as well." She stuck her tongue out at Faramad and Tiamaned before flopping dramatically onto her bedroll.

Suleima gathered her supplies and walked to the mouth of the cave. She refilled her powers then leaned heavily on Gage as exhaustion threatened to drop her in her place.

Suleima awoke with a start. Gage's heavy arm lay across her and silence reigned. She scanned the darkened cave and found everyone where she expected.

Gage's arm tightened around her, and he mumbled, "Go back to sleep."

Unease crept over her. She tightened her hand over his and shook her head slightly. With her other hand, she reached out and slowly tugged on her pack, pulling it in front of where Koa lay nestled by Gage's other arm, which acted as her pillow. Careful not to disturb the bag much, she reached inside and grabbed the piece of fabric from her childhood.

It hummed. She couldn't hear it, not audibly, but the vibration traveled up her arm.

"What's happening?" Gage asked. "I feel that."

Suleima sat up slowly, not wanting to disturb Koa or the others. Gage stood with her, keeping his hand on her arm. She took a few steps forward, shaking her head when Tiamaned opened his mouth to speak. Stopping at the border of her ward, Suleima laid the cloth against the barrier. The fabric sparked and jumped at the connection. Drawing her hand back down, she clutched the cloth tighter in her fist.

Putting her back to the barrier, Suleima stared into the pitch blackness of the cavern beyond. The vibration in her hand suddenly became a pulse and a spark of light appeared just beyond the ward she faced. She retraced her steps to her bedroll and, tucking the cloth into her pocket, Suleima grabbed her bow and approached Kaly.

"I'm heading deeper into the cavern. I want everyone to stay here until I return."

Gage stepped up behind her. "You will *not* go out on your own."

"You can come. But everyone else needs to stay." She turned to face him. "This is no different than Mount Lucent. If you come with me, I call the shots."

Gage's lips pressed into a thin line, but he nodded his agreement.

Suleima pressed a quick kiss to his stern lips and took a step past Kaly into the darkness. She immediately nocked an arrow and kept her bow at the ready as they took tentative steps forward.

She couldn't see much in front of her. The gentle pressure of Gage's hand on her back helped her to avoid missteps. The faint light still twinkled and sparked in front of her as it moved increasing the distance between them.

Soon, a melody could be heard above the sound of running water. Gage stiffened. She heard the lilting notes in the air. "It's not the song of a Naiad," Suleima reassured him as the image flashed across her mind. She had no more desire to encounter one of those again than he did.

Rounding a bend in the cavern, light poured from thousands of glittery stones and jewels embedded in the walls of the high-ceilinged chamber. Pinks and blues and purples bounced from stone to stone, reflecting off the water in the center of the chamber. A small creature stood on the shore with a small bucket, collecting the fallen jewels.

Suleima watched as the creature lifted a purple gemstone from the bucket examining it closely. The gemstone lifted from the palm of the creature's hand and floated a moment before zipping forward and planting itself in an empty spot on the wall to the left. The cloth pulsed in her pocket as it had at their camp, amping up when the creature moved yet another gemstone.

Slowly, the creature turned to face them. The tiny cherub smirked at them with cupid bow lips and winked a mischievous, bright blue eye. She set down her bucket, then laughed, exposing her dimples. Light blue freckles seemed lit from within and glowed with her laughter. She rolled forward in a somersault, bouncing to her feet, coming to a stop in front of them, and let out another giggle.

Gage stiffened as Suleima knelt to her level and set her bow on the ground, within her reach, but unthreatening.

Laughing eyes, too large for the face they occupied, blinked at her. The cherub face tilted, examining Suleima curiously before a frown replaced the smile, and a hand reached out, settling on Suleima's cheek.

"Friend lost." The stilted speech had a somber tone, but the musical quality remained.

"Have you seen him?' Suleima asked.

"Nope!" The creature jumped back, giggling. "Wrong question!"

Suleima pushed down her frustration and tried again. "Do you know where the key is?"

"I know not." The giggling returned. "Still wrong."

"Do you know who knows where the key is?"

"Yep!" Her hands clapped together once and the light in the chamber flashed brightly at the movement. Her lilting laugh echoed down the tunnel on the far side of the chamber.

When Suleima lifted her bow and stood to follow the creature, the cloth, still gripped in her hand, buzzed hard—a warning. She didn't move, unwilling to take the first step.

Gage made a move to step in front of her, but Suleima's arm shot out to the side, stalling his progress. He gave her a curious look but stayed where he was, at her side.

Undulating movement in the water drew her attention. There was a narrow shelf surrounding the pool in the center of the chamber. They would have to navigate that shelf if they wanted to follow the creature they just encountered, and they would definitely be within reach of whatever occupied the pool.

As she stepped back, the buzzing in the cloth lessened. The light in the area had dimmed since the small creature ran off, but she could hear the water now slapping against something at the surface, causing the water to ripple outward, tiny waves forcing the water over the shelf and onto the cavern floor.

Bigger movement splashed more water out of the pool and onto the stone floor. Gage pulled her back another step. "We aren't following her without the others."

"We aren't following her at all," she replied.

Chapter 13

Suleima and Gage returned to the front of the cave. Light was just beginning to spill into the mouth of the cave as the sun rose over the horizon. They explained their encounter as everyone packed up.

"What was she?" Dynasira asked.

"Sounds like a symbriole," Faramad answered. "Was there another with her?"

"No."

"They usually travel in pairs. They are particularly fascinated with jewels, and they protect them fiercely," Tiamaned added.

"There was something in the water in the pool of the chamber we were in. It appeared to suck away the light. The darkness was too much for me to make anything out, other than water sloshing over the edges of the pool," Gage responded.

Faramad and Tiamaned looked at one another and turned back to Suleima.

"There was a second one, then. They have several forms."

"Whatever was in the water was *huge,* she was tiny!" Suleima stated.

He shrugged. "I don't know the reasoning behind the forms they take," Tiamaned replied.

Suleima looked around at the now barren mouth of the cave and her friends surrounding her. "Let's get this over with. The only way to Hamanad and the key is through this place."

They headed into the darkness, using flashlights to aid them. Carvings covered the walls of the cavern, beautiful and intricate. Hidden in the darkness before, Suleima slowed to study the symbols and pictures along the way. Colors popped, a sharp contrast to the grays, browns, and blacks of the natural stone walls. A kraken-like creature depicted reminded Suleima of the creature in the water she and Gage encountered in the chamber with the jewels. A winged goat was next, followed by a cherub.

"Those are the most known forms of the symbriole," Faramad commented, examining the images as well.

"Are there others?" she asked.

Tiamaned shrugged again, "I don't know anyone who knows for sure. They are a trickster type. They hide much of their lore, to protect themselves, I believe."

"Does any of this feel familiar, Tiam?" Dynasira asked.

He shook his head sadly. "No, it doesn't."

"Let's keep moving," Suleima said, changing the subject quickly. "The chamber we found is just ahead. Keep your eyes peeled."

The grand chamber came into view a few moments later. The lights from their flashlights bounced around the room reflected from gemstone to gemstone. Bursts of color danced along the walls. The lights spun and shifted with every movement of the flashlight beams.

"Anyone else feel like they are standing inside a disco ball?" Dynasira asked.

Suleima laid her hand on Dynasira's arm, stalling any further comments. Out in the water, something big and black bobbed with whatever current ran through it. If she hadn't known better, Suleima would have said it was just a log or a naturally formed stone island.

Slowly, an eye blinked open. The whites of the sizable eye became more visible as the enormous black pupil contracted quickly, adjusting to the light of the flashlights. One of its gigantic tentacles lifted, slapping down near the edge of the shelf surrounding the water. Knowing full well the tentacle could reach much further than it had, Suleima backed up several steps, keeping the group behind her.

Nadiram directed her flashlight at the tunnel the symbriole had taken earlier.

"That's where she went," Suleima confirmed. "But we can't get there without getting close to the kraken-thing. Now that we have the flashlights, I can see two more tunnels, but they are both too close to the pool." She shined her flashlight in each of the tunnels.

A giggle echoed.

Suleima took a step back, bringing the whole group with her. She swung her flashlight around looking for another way.

Kaly touched her arm and pointed. "What's over there?"

Directly in front of the tunnel they used to get into the chamber was a strange shadow.

Suleima stepped to the side, shining her flashlight directly at the shadow. Nothing moved, so she stepped closer, Gage on her heels.

It was another opening.

She led them in that direction. A piercing wail reverberated along the walls, so loud it nearly dropped the wolves to their knees.

"She knows we've found another way, I guess," Suleima said, wincing at the pain it caused to her much less sensitive ears. She tried reaching out with her senses to find the other symbriole, but something about the cavern walls was blocking her ability to see anything beyond the tunnel they occupied. Even within the chambers, she found it difficult to suss out the location of anyone in their party with the use of her magic.

The walls in this tunnel were covered with colored, glassy stones as well. Keeping the flashlights pointed at the ground to reduce the light bouncing around, they picked their way to the end of the tunnel, which opened up into another chamber. This one had three exit points as well, but luckily did not include a pool.

This room was barren of gemstones, but rich in carvings. Intricate pictures were once again chiseled into the surface. Suleima recognized a symbol immediately and pointed it out to Tiamaned, Faramad and Nadiram.

"This is the symbol for jinn magic, right?"

Nadiram nodded.

"There are tales we are told from childhood," Tiamaned began. "Long ago, there was said to be a group of jinn who disagreed with the majority and broke off to form their own tribe. Those jinn wished to stay hidden as they were the protectors of artifacts. Some tales say that the jinn who remained wanted to use the power of the artifacts to gain power and dominance. The artifacts were hidden by those in the fractured tribe, and they went into hiding to keep them protected."

Faramad picked up the story. "My father used to tell me those stories. Some of those jinn stuck together, while others took more precious artifacts and scattered them over the world, spreading them out to keep them out of corrupted hands."

"If the key is one of those artifacts..." Suleima started.

"The jinn who separated are protecting it," Nadiram finished.

A loud wail echoed through the cavern, followed by thunderous rumbling, and a choking dust enveloped the group. The wailing traveled from one area to another, but Suleima couldn't see her hand in front of her face. The dust and debris was thick, leaving her gasping for breath.

Pulling at air, Suleima tried to clear the area so they could breathe, but whatever inside this cavern kept her from feeling with her senses stifled her access to her elements as well. With trembling hands, she glided her fae water magic from her core, lifting it into the air. She was unpracticed at using her fae magic without combining it with her shamanistic magic. Going purely by instinct, Suleima released the water above her group, droplets raining down from the ceiling.

The water collected some of the particles of dirt and rock in the air, dropping to the cavern floor in the rain. Clean streaks ran down every face in her group as the water continued to fall.

Coughing, she pulled Gage over to the wall, motioning for everyone else to follow suit. "Anyone injured?" Suleima asked between coughing fits.

Besides the inability to breathe, the group confirmed no one was injured.

Swinging the flashlight again, Suleima noticed the rubble now blocking the tunnel which led back to the pool and another tunnel likely leading back to the same area. "We can't backtrack. Let's keep moving forward. Who wants to guess our next path?"

Faramad stepped forward, wiping the raindrops from his face and succeeding in smearing the filth. "The center tunnel is the clearest. Do we trust it?"

"We don't know what brought down the last tunnel. It's going to be a gamble no matter which one we choose," Gage replied. "I can't smell anything through the dust."

Suleima took Gage's hand and started forward. "The center is as good as any. Let's get moving."

The center tunnel was more like the first, with carvings lining it. More depictions of the symbriole and jinn were interspersed throughout the tunnel.

The air had mostly settled when the tunnel dumped them out into the next chamber. They stopped to wash the grit from their mouths and grab a quick bite. This chamber, like the first, had a pool, but the water inside was eerily still. The walls were not as high and no jewels adorned the surface. The carvings in the chamber were like those in the previous one but less detailed.

Not wanting to stay in one place too long, they pressed on into a new tunnel, choosing one on the right this time. Gemstones were once again embedded in the walls. The air became more oppressive and polluted the further they traveled until they were dumped back out on the soggy floor of the cave with carvings and two collapsed tunnels.

"This must be some sort of maze," Dynasira observed, coughing again. "We are back in the previous chamber."

"We'll go back the way we came—it was shorter—and choose a new exit point," Suleima replied. "Let's get out of this dust as quickly as possible."

Retracing their steps, they spilled back into the room with carvings and reassessed. One of the remaining tunnels had blank walls—no carvings or gemstones. The center one contained more carvings.

"Guesses anyone?" Suleima asked.

"Split up?" Agron suggested. Loud protests from Gage and Dynasira had him backing away with his hands raised. "OK, then. Random draw?"

"Let's try the blank one?" Faramad chimed in.

Suleima nodded and took the lead, but they weren't far before they hit a dead end and had to turn around.

The tunnel with the carvings wound side to side like a snake, with lots of blind turns. Like the chamber it led them from, the carvings weren't as detailed as before. It seemed like an eternity passed before it dumped them out into a new chamber covered once again in gemstones. This chamber, unlike the others, wasn't round. Odd offshoots were carved into the rock, leading nowhere but providing protection from three sides in some places. This chamber had only two routes besides the one they entered from—one with gemstones, the other with carvings. Near the center, a small spring bubbled water up into a tiny basin.

"We should stop here and rest," Gage said. "It must be nearing dark again and we have no idea how long it will take to make it through here. We can set up in this cove and be out of sight." He indicated the deepest cove near the exit with carvings in the walls.

"The water from the spring is fresh. We can refill our canteens from it," Suleima added, dropping her heavy pack into the cove and setting Koa down with the warning not to venture out of sight.

Chapter 14

With Suleima's shamanistic magic hampered by something inside this cavern, she couldn't set a ward around them, so two people would be on guard at all times through the night, even though there was only one direction an enemy could come from. They still had no idea what caused the tunnels to collapse earlier.

She struggled to sleep, and she snuggled in closer to Gage's warmth and security. A squeak in the vast silence was like a bullhorn, and Suleima sat up searching for Koa. He lay snuggled into a wrinkle at the top of her pack, cocooning and cradling him.

Gage got to his feet and shifted.

Kaly sat up and spoke. "Ryan, stay alert, but stay here and keep everyone else with you. We're going to see what that was." She rubbed her eyes and stood, pulling a hunting knife from her pack.

Suleima picked up her bow and crept quietly at Gage's side, Kaly bringing up the rear.

Darkness enveloped them as they left the chamber, the darkness in the tunnel quickly devouring the residual light from the lanterns they left with the group.

A sobbing hiccup and squeak bounced along the walls from the tunnel ahead, and Suleima laid a hand on Gage's scruff, stopping his progress. "I think it is the symbriole we saw earlier." Another heart-wrenching whimper had Suleima moving again, despite Gage's deep growl.

Rounding a bend, there was still no light, but a simple blue glow of freckles was clearly visible.

Kaly switched on a lantern, flooding the tunnel and temporarily blinding Suleima.

When Suleima's eyes adjusted, the symbriole crouched in full view, and her cupid's bow lips pulled back in a snarl, revealing wicked, serrated teeth as she hissed and backed away.

Gage's answering growl had Suleima gripping the hair at his neck, keeping him in place. She slowly knelt beside him and motioned with her other hand for Kaly to do the same. "We aren't here to harm you."

The symbriole hissed with more venom and one of her arms shifted into a thick black tentacle, flashing out and knocking Suleima off balance and into Gage. He snapped at the offending tentacle and must have caught a piece of it because as quickly as it appeared, it vanished. The symbriole's wails increased as she cradled her now injured hand against her chest.

Regaining her balance, Suleima motioned for Gage and Kaly to stay where they were. She lowered herself even further and calmly inched further into the tunnel, closing the distance between her and the symbriole. She felt Gage's outrage at the risk she was taking, but to his credit, he stayed where he was, letting her take the lead.

The symbriole eyed her warily, her breathing heaving and wheezing.

When she was within reach of the cherub-like creature, Suleima sat back on her heels and placed her hands in her lap.

The childlike face alternated between curiosity, fear, and anger. The oversized blue eyes blinked warily as the blue glow from her freckles pulsed.

Suleima laid her hand out palm up and quietly spoke. "I can help to heal your arm." Suleima waited patiently, and slowly she inched closer. At first contact, Suleima reached for her healing power, but it was stifled in the cavern. She turned sad eyes to the symbriole and spoke softly. "My magic doesn't work well in here. There are others with me who can help you heal better. Will you come with us?"

She eyed Gage and Kaly, shying away.

"I promise no more harm to you from us."

The symbriole carefully rose to her full height, not tall enough to reach Suleima's hip if she'd been standing, and took a cautious step forward. She refused to allow Gage or Kaly behind her, halting as soon as she was next to them.

Suleima looked to Gage. "Head back and have Faramad and Tiamaned ready to heal her. We'll be close behind." She ignored the grumbling she felt rather than heard and pointedly looked past him. "Please," she tacked on for good measure, knowing he would be uncomfortable leaving her alone with this unfamiliar creature.

Suleima slowed her pace to match the symbriole's, giving the group time to prepare. "Do you know what happened to the tunnels?"

Tears welled up in her overlarge eyes and her lower lip puffed out. The symbriole reached up with her uninjured hand and pulled on Suleima's sleeve until she stopped and knelt beside her.

The symbriole's face was extremely close to hers and Suleima began to wonder at her sanity to be this close and alone with an unfamiliar creature.

"Touch." The whispered word came just a moment before the symbriole's uninjured hand came up to rest on Suleima's cheek. As if the lantern she kept with her winked out, suddenly Suleima was plunged into pitch blackness. Too close to the tunnel wall to leap away, her panic rose, but a vision slowly came into focus.

Tears fell silently down her cheeks as she felt the bond between this creature and the kraken-like creature in the first chamber. Their bond, like a mating bond, connected them. She felt the anguish and rage of the symbriole for the loss, as keenly as she'd have felt Gage's. The helplessness overwhelmed her as she watched the assault through her bond's eye.

Solisa ripped down the first tunnel. There was no mistaking the fiery red hair blowing in its own wind behind the shadowed figure. The second tunnel was brought down by the symbriole kraken in a desperate attempt to keep Solisa from going after its bonded pair.

The vision ripped away as quickly as it came. Gage stood just a foot away with his teeth bared in a vicious snarl. Suleima wiped at the tears streaming down her face and faced him. "I'm not hurt. She showed me what happened to the tunnels. I felt her pain. I'm okay, honest."

Suleima looked up to find Faramad standing behind Gage, a lantern barely chasing the dark away for her to make him out. "They are distant relatives of the barbegazi fae. The ability to project their experiences through visions is shared. My father told me you encountered a barbegazi while looking for the fae."

Suleima nodded and sat back, leaning into Gage; his warmth chasing away the residual unease from the vision she was shown. "Can you help her?" She directed her question to Faramad.

Instead of answering, he lowered himself to the floor and approached the symbriole at her level, working his magic.

"Why can you use your magic, but Suleima's is blocked?" Kaly's voice chimed in from the darkness when Faramad finished.

"A tribe of jinn are responsible for the creation of this cavern," he answered. "They would never limit their own magic use, but the use of others—I wouldn't be surprised." Faramad dropped his gaze to the symbriole, who laid her hand on his. He flinched before getting a far-off look in his eyes. A moment later, he blinked, and his eyes refocused on Suleima. "The red hair. Was that Solisa?" At her affirmation, he continued, "She has my father?"

"See it." The symbriole slapped Faramad's hand to get his attention. She then dropped her chin and began to hum a low note.

Deep inside the crevices of the tunnel, gemstones, like those in the room with the kraken symbriole, began to glow, emitting a soft light and illuminating additional carvings on the walls.

The carvings depicted the jinn tribe Faramad spoke of. If she hadn't been paying close attention to it, Suleima would have missed the subtle movement of the carvings as they played through a scene, the nuanced story coming to life before her eyes.

Chapter 15

THE TRIBE OF JINN was once powerful and unified. They kept order among the magic users of ancient times. A wicked force threatened everything the jinn worked so hard to build. Great storms and famine spread over the whole of the lands. The earth rumbled and pitched. Great geysers of lava spewed from the earth. And people were dying off at an alarming rate. Arguing over whether to snuff out the threat or reform it fractured the tribe. Those jinn, stronger with the magic to disrupt, went out on their own and destroyed the threat without the agreement of the consensus. Believing they were right, the disruptors segregated themselves, packing up and leaving the tribe to form their own, rather than face the consequences of defying the tribal leadership.

The new tribe settled here and began the cavernous maze, desperate to keep safe the jinn who fought beside them. The harpies, already settled in the swamp lands, made a deal with the newcomers for mutual safety. The harpies would stay in the swamplands, a barrier between the tribe of jinn and the others they divorced themselves from. Each would warn the other of incoming threats.

Once completed, the jinn abandoned the cavern maze settling in the land just beyond the other side. They welcomed the symbrioles into the cave system, who taught them how to light the way through with the gemstones and crystals they embedded in the walls. They would be an extra layer of protection against any who would attempt to reach the artifacts the jinn hid inside.

Suleima stepped back, stunned. "The book—the one Solisa has—it's been used before. It split the jinn tribe when some of them banded together to stop whatever wielded the power of the book. Now it makes sense that they would be the protectors of the key. If they remain here, the jinn will be somewhere close by, once we reach the other end of this maze."

She paused, watching the carvings dance across the walls with light from the jewels tucked into crevices highlighting bits and pieces. A small chest, deep in a hole, covered in matching gemstones, winking in the light, caught her attention. The image wavered as a bubble formed around the chest, shrinking to its size then seemed to pull the dirt in around it, filling the hole. A giant slab of rock descended. The impact of it hitting the ground over the hole vibrated the floor beneath her feet, despite it having been placed centuries before. The shock knocked her to the floor and blinding pain speared the back of her head before everything went black.

Fighting to claw her way to the surface despite the temptation to continue floating in peace, Suleima forced her eyes open. Darkness surrounded her and grit scraped at her eyes and lids, blurring her vision. She tightened her grip on the hand holding hers—Gage.

He lowered his forehead to hers, breathing in her scent and relaxing as the worry racing across their bond subsided.

"You hit your head pretty hard," Faramad said. "Get up slowly. I healed your wound, but you may still be dizzy when you stand."

Gage moved behind her, steadying her when she stood.

"The key is somewhere in this cavern system, but I don't know where. It's buried and spelled."

"Should we leave it alone? Is it hidden enough that Solisa couldn't find it?" Kaly asked from somewhere in the tunnel.

"I don't know," Suleima answered, defeat lacing her tone. "Do I believe she will stop looking for it? No. Do I believe we can protect it better than this cavern has over many centuries? I'm not sure. To take a chance either way is dangerous."

The group made their way back to the chamber and settled in, resting. The symbriole accompanied them but stayed on the far side of the chamber. Without discussion, their guards went from two to three.

Suleima snuggled into her bedroll but her mind whirled, back to the pauguk, the nuberu, and the jinn. She knew how to wield fire, Erist made sure of it. But it was coming to call more naturally. The veil of confusion pulled away as a thought gripped her mind—Volos. The son of the Phoenix and Dryad, protectors of the Fire and Earth elements. The first of the werewolves. That had to be it. Her connection with Gage through their bond must strengthen her connection to fire. Their bond made his change nearly as fast as the dragons' now. Somehow her connection with him allowed her to access fire so much easier.

She kept her musings to herself. While it made sense in her mind, she needed to think on it more.

After rest and food, Suleima packed her supplies, tossed her bag onto her shoulder, lifted her bow, and nocked an arrow. Koa perched on her shoulder, she made her way across the cavern to where the symbriole had bedded down. In her place, covered by a cloak lay a pile of stones. The symbriole had vanished.

Dynasira approached. "No one saw her leave."

Suleima nodded but reached out, fingering the cloth of the cloak. She set her pack down and reached inside, pulling out the piece of cloth she had been carrying since finding it in Erist's burnt shell of a house. It was the same material. Suleima carefully folded both pieces of material and placed them in her pack before facing the group.

"Which way now?" Gage asked her.

"This chamber only has two paths beyond the way we entered. The one we took last night, and the one filled with gemstones," she replied. "Any guesses?"

Dim light from an unknown source bounced across the crystals lining the walls in their chamber, colored flashes echoing through the room at random.

"Let's try the path with gemstones," Kaly suggested. "After whatever happened to cause you to fall in the tunnel last night—let's choose the new one."

Suleima adjusted her pack on her back and, with Gage, led the group down the path on the opposite side of their camp.

There wasn't much talking as they traversed the windy tunnel until it dumped them into another chamber, grander than the last with immensely high ceilings and another pool in the center. Albeit a much smaller pool, a constant drip, drip from the ceiling above was its source. Dynasira and Agron headed to different sides of the chamber, holding their lanterns close to the walls. No gemstones were visible, nor any carvings they could make out, but the cave walls glittered, the walls shimmering in the light from their lanterns, undulating in a dance-like movement.

Nadiram lifted her hand to the wall where her light shined and startled away, her eyes wide and terrified as she quickly backed toward the center of the room. "It's not an illusion; the walls are rippling for real!"

As she spoke, Gage pulled her away from the wall she stood closest to. Aware of it now, the walls moved closer still, shrinking the room in all directions. Calling behind her, Suleima pulled on Gage's hand and led them all into the gemstone-covered tunnel right next to the tunnel they used to enter this chamber.

Once again, only gemstones lined these walls, no carvings could be seen, but the long, twisted path took a long time to dump them into another chamber, this one barren and dull. They kept moving through the only other tunnel available, but it narrowed to nothing—a dead end.

Beyond frustrated, Suleima threw her pack to the ground when they backtracked to the barren chamber and paused to eat. "How much longer must we be trapped in this maddening place?"

Everyone in the chamber stopped what they were doing. Dynasira stepped forward, but Gage waved her off and guided Suleima over to the edge of the chamber, sitting down and pulling her with him, cocooning her in his embrace.

Despite the calmness she felt flowing from him to her, Suleima's fists were tightly clenched and pounding on her thighs. She wanted to scream, though her voice was barely above a whisper when she spoke. "I'm failing them." She threw her arm out, indicating the others in the cavern. "Failing Hamanad. Failing Erist."

Gage's hand drifted over her back in soothing circles as he turned her chin with his other hand to face him. "You are far from failing any of us."

"My magic is useless in here!"

"And, you've overcome that before." He indicated the bow on the ground beside her and the knife discreetly tucked into her boot. "You don't need your magic to fight."

"We only know the key is here. We don't have any idea where it is or how to get it! And Hamanad could be anywhere. Faramad needs..."

Gage stopped the flood of words with a finger pressed to her lips. "Faramad knows we are doing everything in our power to find his father. No one ever thought the key would just appear, or that Hamanad would be patiently sitting in a sunny spot waiting for us to join him. We are stronger together and we will work as a team to find the key and to find Hamanad."

A harsh bellow echoed from the mouth of the dead-end tunnel, causing Suleima and Gage to jump to their feet. Suleima had her bow ready before Gage shifted. The others were behind and beside her a moment later.

"There was nothing down that tunnel a bit ago and no chambers. How did it get in there?" Tiamaned muttered.

"Gather your things quickly," Suleima said, her gaze and aim never leaving the mouth of the tunnel. "We'll head back, hope the walls stopped moving, and find another way."

"Now!" Kaly shouted, her voice borrowing its command from Gage.

Supplies were shoved into packs and the chamber emptied within moments, everyone heading back down the gemstone-laden tunnel to the glittery cavern, with Gage and Suleima protecting them from the rear.

The sound of heavy steps echoed through the tunnel, getting closer with each step. The harsh bellow sounded again, its timbre weakening Suleima's knees and her head throbbed. She stumbled from the pain, immediately weightless as Gage shifted and lifted her, their positions taken over by Kaly and Ryan. Gage raced with her through the tunnel, moving to the head of the group.

Dumped back into the glittery room, Gage maneuvered across the chamber, avoiding the pool and entering the only other tunnel available. Its walls sparkled like the chamber they just left. A brief pause confirmed that while the walls glittered and undulated like the chamber, the walls of the tunnel did not close in around them.

Once everyone made it into the tunnel, Gage handed Suleima off to Kaly and took her place at the mouth of the tunnel, watching and waiting for whatever bellowed to appear.

Kaly allowed Suleima to wiggle out of her grasp and stand on her own feet but stood blocking her path to the mouth of the tunnel. "Please stay here," Kaly pleaded. "Let him see what is chasing us."

Before Suleima could respond, the floor beneath their feet waved, a giant ocean swell racing down the tunnel and throwing them off balance.

Regaining their footing, Dynasira and Agron each grabbed one of Suleima's arms and led the way, racing away from the glittery room. The tunnel, though longer than any of the others in the cavern, passed by in a blur, dumping them into a plain rock chamber with a wide, short tunnel on the opposite side. The brightness of the sun outside made Suleima squint. The sudden stillness of the floor since leaving the tunnel caused her to stumble again.

Heedless of whatever could be outside the cavern, Suleima righted herself and made a beeline for the mouth of the cave. She hadn't noticed the anxiety threatening to halt her inside the cavern until she finally gasped in a lungful of fresh air in the bright meadow beyond.

Chapter 16

THE DAMPENING EFFECT OF the cavern gone, and her powers reawakening, Suleima's whole body tingled, and she marveled at the rush. She spun on her heel and pulled up a ward in front of the cavern opening the moment Gage, bringing up the rear, cleared the entrance. Suleima sat hard on the ground, scanning the area with her senses and finding only natural wildlife in their vicinity.

Gage quietly spoke with Kaly and Dynasira before joining Suleima, taking her hand in his, grounding her.

They sat silently for a bit before he spoke. "What is the next step?" Her unease likely blazed over their bond, he immediately pulled her closer.

Tears welled in her eyes unbidden, her voice barely above a whisper. "I don't know. I can't lead this. I just don't know." She tried to grasp at her confidence, hang on to any shred of it remaining, but it slipped out of her reach and the tears fell in earnest. He tightened his hold on her, shifting so she was more comfortable, and held her while she cried, his hand absently running up and down her spine.

She calmed slowly, drinking in the peace and serenity he emoted through their bond, and straightened, wiping away the tears remaining.

Gage tipped her chin with his fingers, their eyes meeting, and lay his hand on her cheek. "One step at a time. We do this together. You can do it. With each of us right alongside. Just one more step."

Suleima closed her eyes, pulled in a hiccupping breath, and did her best to chase away the lingering fear and doubts. She opened her eyes when a tug at her long braid caught her attention.

After releasing her braid, Koa patted the side of her neck with his hand and snuggled in close. His tiny show of support warmed her and made her smile.

She met Gage's eyes again. "This tribe of jinn has been protecting the key for centuries. We find them first. When we meet up with them, we lay out what is happening, and together, we'll figure out the best course of action. I cannot justify trying to unearth the key without consulting with its protectors first." She turned to the rest of the group. "Getting it with their help will be much easier than fumbling through that cavern blindly."

Dynasira nodded once and picked up her pack. "Which way?"

She looked around at the group preparing to follow her lead once again. Her fears rose to the surface, threatening to swallow her. As each of them locked eyes with her, she saw the confidence they had in her.

Gage lowered his forehead to hers and closed his eyes for a moment before speaking. "You were chosen to lead the council for a reason. You have led before, no matter how reluctantly, and we have all been better for it. We have confidence in you. Now it is your turn to have confidence in yourself."

Suleima closed her eyes again and reached out with her senses. She scanned as far as she could reach and perceived nothing out of the ordinary. A wave of calm from Gage allowed her to focus when her frustration rose. It was the 'nothing' she focused on. Her brow furrowed and Gage's finger rested on the wrinkle she knew appeared there. When he started to pull back, because she relaxed her brow, Suleima held his hand in place. She scanned again. And again. Slowly opening her eyes, she lowered Gage's hand but kept it wrapped in hers. With her other hand, Suleima pointed into the woods off to the west of the cavern. She smiled. "There's nothing over there. Nothing. My magic blurs right over it. I think that's where they are."

They approached the boundary of the area blurred in her senses. The trees were dense, hindering vision.

Kaly approached the group. "Their disruption is powerful. I don't scent any fresh smells, other than the foliage and water nearby. In wolf form though, Gage can smell a lot of people directly in front of us."

Suleima faced the group, "Gage and I will go in first. The rest of you, hold here. They likely have the power to disrupt any shield I create. Let us check it out. Kaly will let you know when it is safe to follow."

Without waiting for a response, Suleima headed toward the area where she suspected the jinn to be hiding.

The trees became denser, before abruptly opening into a meadow. Suleima's ears popped as she crossed the boundary of the trees, revealing a quaint village of log homes, smoke lazily drifting from the chimneys of a few of them. Curtains in a few of the homes slammed closed, a few locks turning audibly.

Suleima's palm itched to pull her bow from where it rested around her back. She flexed her hand instead.

Gage's hackles rose, but no snarl appeared on his lips.

At the center of the village, a lone door swung open, and a deep voice boomed from the darkness within. "Leave now."

"My friends and I need your help. A fae is coming for the key you protect. We want to stop her from getting the key which she intends to use to enslave all beings. She already has the book of spells the key opens."

"I said *leave*!" A quaver in the voice belied the nervousness of the jinn.

"We wish no harm among you or your people. A friend of ours, a jinn from another tribe, went missing. We also search for him."

"If this fae has the book, you cannot help your *friend*." The voice held disdain.

Suleima gasped. "You know where Hamanad is?" When no response came, Suleima scanned the village, sensing something familiar, but odd in the home the voice boomed from. "He's here, isn't he?"

A scuffle behind her registered, momentarily pulling her attention. Through their bond, Gage showed her Kaly and Ryan holding Faramad and Nadiram back as they tried to get closer.

"His son, his apprentice, and a friend from his tribe are here to help us find him. Please release Hamanad so he may reunite with his loved ones." Suleima took a few steps forward, motioning to Gage to stay put. She removed her bow and lay it in front of Gage, ignoring his low growl, before standing and continuing toward the house slowly.

"Stay where you are!" the depth of the voice changed, becoming a shrill squeal.

She slowed but did not stop. About twenty feet from the house, her magic fell away, out of reach, exactly as it had when Nadiram shook her hand. Suleima's step faltered at the emptiness, and Gage growled behind her. She stepped forward again, "I won't hurt you. I only wish to see my friend."

With her magic gone, Suleima couldn't determine where in the house the voice was coming from, or where Hamanad was. The darkness swallowed her the moment she stepped over the threshold. Gage howled his disapproval, but Suleima knew he would stay where she left him, for now.

The cool metal of a knife against her throat stopped her movement, but she tamped down her fear, unwilling to be the cause of Gage attacking. She dropped the knife, which she'd tucked in her sleeve when she dropped her bow to the ground, into her hand, gripping the handle tightly and shifting her arm, so it rested at her assailant's abdomen. "I am no threat to you unless you make me. And my friends will be a problem if you harm me. I only wish to see Hamanad."

"You cannot help him. We haven't harmed him. We protect him." It was a quiet female voice she heard now.

"Please allow me to see him. I only wish to help protect him."

Slowly, light filled the room. In front of her lay a stone statue on a canvas litter. Hamanad.

"We did not do this to him. We brought him here for safekeeping," the woman with dark hair said as she tentatively lowered the knife from Suleima's throat. She kept it up ready to defend herself.

Suleima bent to tuck her knife back into its sheath, then stood, keeping her hands visible and her movements small. "What happened to him?"

"A powerful fae spell."

"You and your tribe cannot disrupt it?" she asked.

The woman shook her head.

Suleima froze at Gage's howl. Hands still up, she backed toward the doorway until the darkness filled the interior and she could see the surrounding village outside again.

Kaly held Suleima's bow and the rest of the group formed a circle, their backs to each other, ready for a fight.

Her gaze connected first with Gage, then Kaly before she returned to the small house, to Hamanad's stone form, confident her friends would stand watch, but allow her the freedom to handle the situation. "How long has he been like this? How long will he survive like this?"

The jinn looked at Hamanad's form before answering. "The harpies brought him to us a few weeks ago."

"The harpies did this?"

A sharp and aggressive expression appeared on her face instantaneously, her knife raising again. "They *brought* him to us. The harpies would not do this, even if they had the ability."

"Okay, then who? How? And how do we fix this?" With effort, Suleima relaxed her posture and leaned against a chair, attempting to defuse the tension threatening to choke her. Gage's irritation buzzed over the bond, ready to react to whatever made her uncomfortable, and the last thing they needed was him reacting aggressively.

The woman swung her gaze to Hamanad before turning back to Suleima. "He is jinn?"

Suleima nodded. "He is. He is my friend."

"You are not jinn."

"No. I am a shaman. We have come a long way to find him and to help protect the key."

"You travel with wolves."

"And dragons," Suleima added. "We also have three jinn with us who know and love Hamanad." She relaxed the tension in her shoulders before continuing. "Inside the caverns, the carvings moved." She continued, describing the images the carvings showed.

Shock registered across the woman's face as Suleima spoke. She was pensive for a moment, then motioned Suleima to precede her out the door.

Meeting Gage and the others in the center of the clearing Suleima turned to Tiamaned, Faramad, and Nadiram. "Hamanad is inside. He is held in a spell like a statue."

"Can I disrupt the spell?" Nadiram asked.

"No. We have all tried. It requires a spell from the book your friend says the fae have. You are jinn?"

Shyly, Nadiram nodded her head.

The woman paused, her expression pensive, then spoke. "Come inside, all of you."

She led the way into the house and directed them to sit down. Faramad stopped at his father, placing his hand on the stone, and bowed his head. Tiamaned and Nadiram took their places beside him. All eyes turned to the woman.

"I am Pila." She turned to where Suleima sat, next to Gage's wolf. "If the cavern has shown you its carvings, its magic believes you to be safe. I will tell you what I can. The key you search for is ancient. The book it opens is capable of horrific things."

"Why has the book not been destroyed?" Tiamaned interrupted.

Pila faced Suleima when she answered. "Yes, the book is capable of immense destruction, but it also holds spells of great power and healing." She turned to Tiamaned. "Like the spell to free this jinn from the stone prison encasing him." She paused a moment, listening. "The key has been hidden for centuries. The book was lost through time. You say a fae has possession of it?"

"Yes. A powerful fae, the Sun Goddess, possesses the book."

"How did she acquire it?"

"From what we have learned, the book was in the possession of a shaman, a power-hungry shaman. Upon his death, it was taken by his apprentice, Dirrin. After his death, Solisa sent an energy vampire, Kylin, into Dirrin's camp to retrieve the book and bring it to her. I encountered Solisa outside the cavern and, because of her, half of a symbriole pair was killed inside the cavern. She will not stop until she finds the key. I believe she plans to use the same spells from the book your jinn ancestors fought against before they left their known jinn tribe to bring the key here and hide."

"She harmed a symbriole within the walls of the cavern? Urlanta? Or Lyrtic?" Pila's voice trembled.

"Urlanta? Lyrtic? Are those the symbriole pair?" At Pila's confirmation, Suleima continued, "The one killed was in her kraken form. Neither gave us their names when we encountered them."

"The cavern is protected from magic."

"My magic was hampered within. The jinn traveling with us were unaffected. And it seems Solisa was unaffected as well."

Pila pulled an old tome from the top of an old and very dusty shelf, placing it on the table near Suleima. Flipping the book open, Pila thumbed through the pages until she came upon a page with a map.

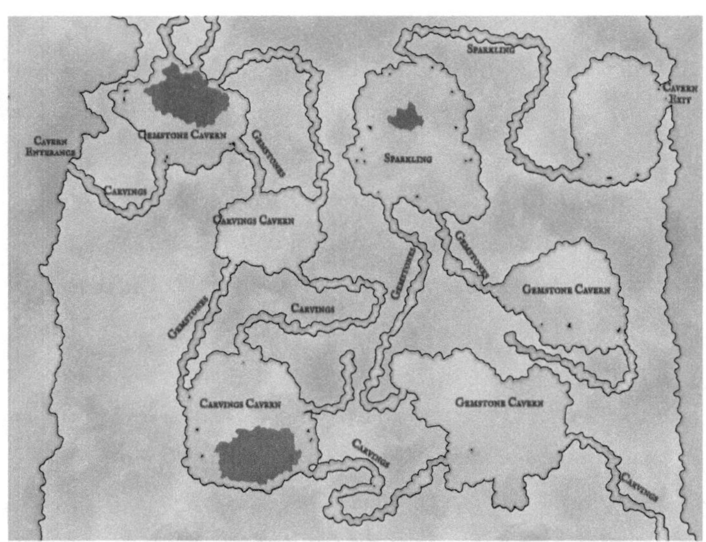

"That's the cavern we were in," Kaly said, looking over Suleima's shoulder at the map.

Pila nodded. "The first of the jinn to come here used their magic to create the caverns. This is why only the jinn were able to access their magic inside. I do not know how or why this Solisa person was able to use their magic inside." She turned a few more pages stopping at a drawing of a book and, next to it, an ornate key. "My people have not touched the key since it was hidden. That is one of the reasons it *remains* hidden. The knowledge has been lost to most of the tribe. It is only passed down through our tribe leaders now. As the current Chieftain of this tribe, I am responsible for the key and the well-being of my tribe."

"Solisa is coming for the key. And, we just established she can wield magic within that cavern. How safe is it there with this new information?" Dynasira stepped forward as she spoke. "No one wants Solisa to have access to those spells."

"Up until now, we have been under the impression that only jinn could use magic there, and with the knowledge of the key lost to most, there was no danger in leaving the key where it has been for centuries. With this new information, now I am not so sure." Pila glanced at Hamanad's prone form. "Your friend can survive within this spell for about a month more. You will need not only the key but also the book if you have any hope of saving him." Pila's head lowered solemnly. "Once, long ago, before the jinn tribe splintered, the book would not be necessary. Over the many generations, our power has diminished. Growing weaker with each generation, as I imagine has happened with the half of the tribe who stayed in our ancestral lands, the jinn alive here today would no longer have the power to create the great cavern maze you traversed.

"We have accepted the loss of power. We live in harmony with the creatures and nature surrounding us, choosing to isolate and live in peace."

Chapter 17

WHILE PILA GATHERED HER own supplies, Suleima sent the others to rest, and recharged her magic. Soon, Pila left another jinn in charge in her place and they set off back toward the cavern. The skies, overcast and gloomy, drizzled a misty rain, dampening everything and bringing a chill to Suleima. She rubbed her arms, hoping the friction would help to warm her, but the dampness from her long-sleeved shirt only served to increase her shivers.

Exhaustion from the stress and physical toll of their journey didn't help as the cold sapped even more of her energy, her eyes threatening to slam shut. She caught herself after stumbling and paused to look back at the group. Only Pila acted perfectly alert. Even the wolves and dragons were showing signs of slowing.

Once they reached the mouth of the cavern, the ward she placed when they exited was still intact and undisturbed. "Can you sense if the key has been tampered with?"

Pila gave a small nod. "It is still in hiding. Something is still within the cavern labyrinth, besides the symbriole, but whatever it is has not found the key yet."

Stifling a yawn, Suleima asked, "Will it be safe while we rest a bit? Or must we head directly to it?"

"You will be unable to protect it in your current state. Any of you. We will rest." Pila reached out and laid her hand on the ward. "You should rest inside where it will be warmer and drier."

Suleima pulled down the ward before leading the way back inside the massive corridor leading to the last chamber of the cave system. After ensuring everyone was settled, she curled up against the chamber wall, snuggling in tight to Gage. Her eyes kept slamming shut until she couldn't fight it anymore.

Suleima fought to open her eyes. Her entire body felt weighted down. With effort, she turned her head, finding Gage, no longer in wolf form sleeping next to her. As her eyes traveled across the tunnel, every person, including Pila, was soundly asleep. She strained to move her arm and shifted Koa closer to Gage. Sweat poured off of her as she struggled to sit up. The exertion required to get to her knees had her panting. Something wasn't right. She nudged Gage, but he barely stirred. Calling his name had no effect either. Suleima pushed to her feet and laid a hand on the wall to steady the pronounced sway while her equilibrium settled. "Dyna?" She reached over and shook her friend, but she got no response from her either.

Becoming frantic, Suleima went to each of her companions in turn, but no one reacted to her. She stumbled back out of the mouth of the cavern, looking around desperately to find—what? She didn't know. Nothing outside caught her attention, but she was more alert. The instant she crossed the threshold of the cavern again, tiredness overwhelmed her.

Suleima struggled to keep her eyes open as she grabbed Gage under his arms and heaved. When she was a few feet from the entrance, she pulled on earth to aid in bringing him back into the wooded area. Each time she returned to the cavern, exhaustion pulled at her, but by the time she'd pulled Dynasira and Kaly out of the cave, Gage had begun to stir.

As she laid Ryan next to Kaly, Gage burst to his feet, alert and in fight mode.

"Shh." Suleima laid a hand on his shoulder. "There is no direct threat I sense. You are safe. Kaly and Ryan are safe. I am safe. Whatever is causing the exhaustion is wearing off out here. But, when anyone re-enters the cave, it comes back full force." She handed him a canteen. "Some water will help. I'll pull Nadiram next. Maybe she can disrupt whatever is happening in there."

Gage's growl was present as he spoke, "Do not go back in there. Whatever that spell is doing, it's dangerous."

She laid her hand on his cheek. "I need you to sit here and drink and recover, so you can help me bring the rest out."

He grabbed her arm, stopping her from turning away. "We didn't feel this way on the way out."

"We were only in that section a short time on the way out. I don't know if we were in there long enough to feel any effects. Or it could be new. We won't know until I get Pila out and ask her if it is normal."

"If she's out, too..."

"I know. Stay here and keep the others from losing it as they come to."

It spoke to how out of it he still was that Gage didn't argue, only sat down hard next to his packmates.

Suleima brought Nadiram out and set her next to Gage, before returning for Pila. By that time, Dynasira was up and moving, helping to pull Agron and the other jinn out into the fresh air and sunlight.

Suleima handed out fresh water and crouched in front of Pila and Nadiram. After Pila told them she was unaware of any spells or defenses on the cavern system which would have put them to sleep, Suleima turned to Nadiram. "Can you disrupt whatever that magic is? And can you tell what kind of magic it is?"

"I can try." Nadiram stood, brushed off her loose tan trousers, and flexed her fingers before approaching the cave.

Silence reigned outside of the mouth of the cave as Nadiram approached, laying her fingers on the wall at the edge of the opening.

The smell of ozone and the sensation of ears popping followed, and Nadiram jerked back her hand, cradling against her. She was out of breath when she replied, "I think whatever it was is gone now. It wasn't jinn. Beyond that, I can't tell much."

Suleima walked her over to Faramad and Tiamaned, who were beginning to rouse themselves, so they could heal her.

"It wasn't a jinn spell. Can you sense the key still, Pila?"

Pila ventured into the mouth of the cave and a faraway look drifted over her face. A moment later, it shifted to alarm. "It's not in hiding any longer!"

Suleima bolted down the tunnels she remembered. The glittery walls in the chamber with the small pool in the center vibrated in what seemed like—anger? The walls weren't closing in this time though, only sharp undulations, bouncing light around the room erratically. The light bounced oddly off one section of the room and Suleima slid across the floor to it. The symbriole was curled in a ball, unresponsive.

Suleima scanned the room with her eyes, her magic still useless within the walls of the cavern. The other trips through this room had been quick, first with the walls closing in, then being chased by—who knows what. But, as she looked around the room, one thing became very clear: this room hid the key.

The edges of the room were packed dirt and stone like the rest of the cavern, but the center of the floor housed what used to be a huge slab of stone. The stone slab she saw in her vision. Now, however, cracks ran in every direction, dividing it into large and small chunks. Reaching her hand down into one such crevice, the texture of the rough stone took on a glassy, smooth texture, suggesting extreme heat was responsible for the damage.

Suleima reached forward but jerked her hand back as if it had been burned. An odd glow surrounded the symbriole.

Realizing she was no longer alone in the room, Suleima reached back to Dynasira. "I need the cloth out of my pack, the larger one." Dynasira gave her a puzzled look but pulled the largest piece from the pack and handed it to Suleima. At least Dynasira had thought ahead and brought Suleima's supplies, instead of running blindly down the tunnels into the unknown.

"Why?" Dynasira asked.

"I..." she began. She paused, her head tilting to the side. "It feels right? That's the best answer I have." She held up her hand. "I can't touch her."

Suleima wrapped the cloth around the symbriole, careful to keep the fabric between their skin. Then gathered her close and lifted.

"Let's get her out of the cavern to Faramad." Suleima led the way, carrying the symbriole, who was heavier than she looked.

Gage met them halfway down the glittery tunnel but turned when he saw them, leading the way back out.

Once back in the sunlight, Suleima rushed to Faramad, a cup of water cradled in his hand. She set the symbriole down next to him. "Careful, there's something coating her. It burned."

Faramad gave her a puzzled look. "I touched her before, when I healed her arm. I felt nothing then."

Pila stepped up to them. "She must have tried to protect the key." She sat down next to the symbriole and placed her hand above the surface of her skin. "The key was hidden, but not only that, there are protections woven into it, onto it. It cannot be touched by bare hands without severe burns. It seems the key's protections transferred onto the symbriole."

Nothing visibly changed, but when Pila removed her hand, the cloth covering the symbriole floated open and away from her body. Pila nodded to Faramad. "It is safe now."

Faramad placed a hand over the side of her head where blood still oozed and worked his healing magic.

Suleima paced back and forth, waiting for the symbriole to wake. It wasn't until Gage's hand closed over her left forearm that she stopped. She gave him a puzzled look as he walked, pulling her along, only stopping when they stood next to Tiamaned.

"Faramad is busy with the symbriole. Are you awake enough to help with Suleima?"

"What?" she asked, confused as Gage guided her to sit beside Tiamaned. Then, she noticed. The skin on her left palm was blackened where she had touched the symbriole. With all of the scarring, she never even noticed the damage.

Tiamaned gently took her hand in his and worked his magic. Beyond the slightest cooling sensation, she felt nothing else.

As he finished, Pila sat beside them. "I have failed to protect the key. With the key and the book, this fae you spoke of will have untold power. She can destroy anything and everything if she chooses."

"Do you have any way to track the key, in the event it was taken?" Suleima asked.

"It was never supposed to leave the cavern, never supposed to be uncovered. For centuries, we have kept it hidden in this labyrinth."

The symbriole silently approached them, a slight limp to her walk, but beyond that, there was no evidence she had been harmed. Placing her hand on Suleima's cheek, the symbriole gave a sad smile.

Suleima closed her eyes and was transported back into the cavern, in the glittery room, with the symbriole. With Solisa.

Suleima and her friends were so focused on getting out, getting away, they never noticed the fae standing in a darkened crevice of the glittery room. Solisa's hands worked, waving and pulsing. The magic she worked, influencing their decisions, making them run, rather than fight. Hiding Solisa from their view as they raced, chased by nothing but a sound and magic.

As their group passed into the glittery tunnel on their way out of the cavern, Solisa stepped away from her hiding spot, a smug grin on her face. She continued to wave her hands, the bellow following their group and echoing through, continuing the chase.

The fae attempted to use her magic again, but nothing was happening. She screamed her frustration and stomped on the floor in an oddly child-like temper tantrum.

The symbriole stayed quiet, watching the woman stomp around the room, jerking her arms and hands around frantically. Using small movements to keep her location concealed, the symbriole flicked her fingers and listened as several gemstones fell from the tunnel walls leading back to the beginning of the caverns.

Solisa stopped and curled her lips in a snarl. Pulling her hands up, as if ready to conjure, she backtracked through the cavern's tunnel system. Every time it seemed the fae would dismiss the sound and turn back, the symbriole dropped more stones, enhancing their echoes to draw the fae further and further from the glittery room. Whatever was in that room, the fae woman shouldn't have it.

She kept Solisa busy for several hours, making noises or disorienting her by conjuring illusions which looked like new tunnels.

Reaching a chamber, not as deep in the bedrock as the others, Solisa's magic grew more powerful, and she cackled before lighting the chamber with her fire, so brightly, it may as well have been sunlight. The symbriole squinted against the bright light.

A spell book materialized, seemingly out of thin air, and glowed, pulsing erratically. She held it aloft and slowly spun around, stopping where it pulsed the fastest. Absolute glee shined on her face, and she dropped the bright light and focused on the luminescence of the book.

The symbriole raced back to the glittery room as fast as she could. She could sense the fae's movement, and by the time Solisa returned, she was well hidden in the shadows and crevices of the chamber.

Solisa, oblivious to the symbriole who crouched at the far side of the room, took a few steps forward, swinging the book and watching the glow's ebb and flow. Taking slow steps, she swung the book from side to side, adjusting her direction until she stood at the edge of the small pool, the book's glow was blinding in the darkness of the chamber.

The fae pulled the book to her chest and raced toward the exit.

The symbriole kept up, but maintained her distance and watched the fae work magic again. This time, she laid some curse over the mouth of the cavern. The symbriole could hear and sense the group from before as they re-entered the caverns. But, as Solisa left the area to return to the glittery chamber, the symbriole was forced to retreat, quickly finding a new hiding place as the fae returned to the pool.

The symbriole's uneasy feeling grew. She needed to stop the nasty fae with the fiery hair. She shifted, her four powerful hooves quiet on the cavern floor; her perspective changing as she was now head and shoulders taller than the fae woman; the fae who killed her pair. Her own bellow outmatched the one Solisa conjured with her magic. Rearing, the goat-like hooves of the symbriole connected with Solisa's arm. Her grunt of pain echoed off the walls and she cradled her injured arm against her ribs.

Solisa's head snapped around, and her magic swelled, somehow pulling from the power within the book she held.

The symbriole managed one more good kick before Solisa swung the book, connecting with the symbriole's head, dropping her where she stood.

Pain flashed through the blackness as the symbriole opened her eyes. The fae clawed at the ground, hair swaying in front of her face. The pool of water had dried up at some point. The great stone covering the floor in this section of the cavern was hot to the touch, cracked and shattered. Steam rose from the cracks as the water beneath evaporated in the heat the stones gave off. The heat generated by the fae woman.

Solisa scraped the ground with her nails, cursing under her breath about her magic not working to make the digging unnecessary. She hissed and jerked her hand back, the tips of her fingers blackened.

The symbriole twisted, and with all of her strength, aimed another kick with her hooved feet at the fae, catching her shoulder and knocking her away from where the pool had been.

A blast of pain seared the symbriole from the inside, who cried out at the unbearable burning sensation. As the darkness claimed her again, the symbriole shifted in hopes of healing the damage Solisa inflicted.

Chapter 18

SULEIMA BLINKED OUT OF the vision. Everyone stood around her, waiting for—something. She turned to Pila. "Solisa has the key," she said simply.

Everyone began talking at once, and Suleima held her hand up to stop them. "The jinn should stay here. Stay with Hamanad. Kaly, Ryan, and Jonah should stay too. Dyna, can you and Agron fly us out of here?"

Dynasira nodded, jumping to her feet and gathering her pack.

Suleima turned to Pila. "I'm leaving my wolves and jinn in your protection, and *for* your protection. Keep Hamanad safe. We will get the key and the book back from Solisa." She raised her hand to stop Kaly's protest. "You need to be here. You can relay our progress to the others. You can alert the rest of the pack if things go wrong. Protect Pila and the rest. We are counting on you."

Suleima and Gage grabbed their packs and approached the now-shifted dragons. "Take us to Zenisa. She needs to know, and we need to see if she will keep her word and help."

Gage stopped her, taking her hand in his. "Koa?"

Suleima looked at the fae hanging tight to her pack strap. "He's coming."

Gage squeezed her hand before dropping it.

Before they knew it, they were weightless and soaring over the clouds, clutched in the talons of two enormous dragons.

The ground rushed by in a blur, the air chilling by the minute as they got closer and closer to the snowy mountain where Zenisa resided. Suleima was chilled to the bone by the time Dynasira and Agron landed. She tried to keep her teeth from chattering as she unfolded her stiff joints. The bone-deep ache in her scarred left arm brought tears to her eyes.

Gage caught her as she stumbled on her first step. "You ok?"

"Just cold." Suleima repositioned her pack and started up the path to Zenisa's door.

Zenisa stepped out before they reached the porch, her silky blue gown blowing in the wind. She must have seen something in their demeanor, because her eyes widened and she stepped back, motioning for them to enter her home.

Closing the door behind them, Zenisa directed them to a deep cherry dining room table big enough to sit a whole host of people. "What happened?" she asked, a steaming pot of tea in her hand, where none had been a moment ago.

"Solisa found the key," Suleima answered. "Now she has both the book and the key, and we have no idea what the next step is. We found

Hamanad, the jinn. She spelled him into a statue. We need the book and key to heal him."

Zenisa's eyes widened, and she stepped back, wind that only existed for her blowing her hair back. Her eyes narrowed, and her lips pulled back in a sneer. "You didn't tell me about your new friend." There was a chill to Zenisa's voice which hadn't been there since their encounter after Zia's death.

Gage tightened his muscles, ready to defend her.

She laid her hand on his forearm to halt him. "Koa came about as a result of whatever magic you performed to make Zia's moonflowers grow so quickly. I found him after you returned here. I went to visit Zia's memorial, just before I left to find Hamanad."

Her icy eyes appeared to glow with her anger. "You dared to keep him secret from me? I ended The Green Knight. His return didn't seem worth mentioning?"

"There wasn't time," Suleima answered without inflection. She turned her shoulder, where Koa perched, away from Zenisa. "Koa is not Alder. He's a child. Raised to care about others, to have empathy and compassion, I believe he will thrive and not live in the violence and hatred of his sire."

"We aren't here to discuss Koa," Dynasira chimed in. "We don't have time for this. Solisa has the key. Did you miss that? We need to find her. Can you help us with *that*? Will you help us against her?"

Zenisa's narrowed eyes swung over to Dynasira, but Suleima stood. "We aren't going to get anywhere if we are fighting amongst ourselves. I am taking care of Koa. If you want further discussions on the matter, it will have to wait. For now, do you know how we can find Solisa before she destroys the world as we know it?"

Zenisa looked ready to argue, but her demeanor shifted in the blink of an eye.

Suleima eyed her warily, uneasy at the quick shift, but she would need her help if they had any hope of finding Solisa before it was too late.

Gage stepped up behind her, placing his hand on the small of her back, likely sensing her unease. He remained quiet, allowing her to lead this conversation.

"Do you have a way to locate Solisa? Or do you know where she might have gone?" Suleima asked, keeping her tone calm and forcing her body to relax.

"Was she alone when she found the key?"

"She did send a pauguk and a nuberu at us during the journey, but when I saw her, she was alone," Suleima replied. "The visions inside the caverns—she was alone too."

"You're having visions now?" Zenisa asked, one eyebrow arched.

"No. We encountered a symbriole pair in the cavern. Solisa killed one of the pair. The other showed me visions of her encounters with Solisa inside the cave."

Surprise evident on her face, Zenisa replied, "Symbrioles are rare. I was unaware there were any nearby."

"There are several fae types in the area, protectors of and protected by the jinn tribe who live there. They do not wish to be part of fae society." Suleima couldn't say that for sure, but she didn't like the greedy look passing over Zenisa's face at the mention of the symbrioles. She changed the subject quickly, pulling out the piece of fabric from her backpack. The silky fabric hummed as her fingers drifted gently over its surface. She tilted her face up, looking Zenisa in the eye before speaking. "This fabric of my mother's was given to Erist when I was sent with him. It seems to buzz with warning and is a protection against magic. When the key's protections would've caused burns, this fabric saved me from harm."

Zenisa's laugh was mirthless. "That fabric isn't your mother's. It never was. Vorelar, the barbagazi who helped care for you—it belonged to him. Barbegazi and symbrioles are closely related. Their magic works in similar ways. They can share their memories with others using their visions, and some are even able to show visions of things yet to happen. They are often weavers, and imbue their magic into the cloth. Vorelar created the piece of fabric you hold for you. It is attuned to you, and likely the reason you can sense warnings from it," Zenisa said, dismissively waving her hand. "How did you manage to get rid of the pauguk?"

"We separated his bones and turned them to ash," Dynasira responded.

"That would have to be a damn hot fire," she observed, eyeing Suleima. "How did you manage such a feat??

"Do we have time for this chat?" Agron interrupted.

Suleima felt a build-up of power from Zenisa and stepped in front of Agron, a shield pulled in front. "Think very hard before you release your magic, Zenisa," Suleima warned. "My friends are off limits. Solisa is the enemy here, and I won't tolerate aggression aimed at someone who was *trying* to help stop Solisa from getting the key while you hid in your ice cave." She took a few calming breaths before continuing. "This is getting off track. We need to focus on what is in front of us. I understand your surprise with Koa. However, you were gone before he was found and there hasn't been a free moment where I could have come to you to speak about it." Against her instincts, Suleima dropped her shield but stayed between Agron and Zenisa. "To answer your question, I used my fire magic to burn hot enough." She glanced at Gage. "There was an ease to pulling the fire I've not had before. I believe Gage's connection to Volos through his wolf form, and my connection through him, allowed me to more easily access that part of my magic."

As Zenisa's magic faded from the room, Suleima retook her seat at the table and waited for Zenisa to do the same.

"Solisa would probably return to her lands to the south before she attempts to open the book. She rarely leaves her lands and the fact she did so, speaks to her desire to have access to the book."

"Where can we find her lands?" Suleima asked.

"Far to the south, beyond the mountains you call home." Zenisa stood and pulled a map from the shelves of the next room, a library full of live-edge wood shelves and bookcases. She spread the map out onto the table and pointed out where Suleima's home would be, then gently traced her finger along the edge of a vast area in the south. "Here is where her lands are. Where she is exactly, I cannot say. Knowing her, I would venture to guess she is somewhere near the center, or further south. Her paranoia would not allow her to live near a border. She would want as much space between her and her borders as possible. No one could sneak up on her that way. One of her many minions would be sure to report any threats well before they reached her."

Suleima looked to Dynasira and Agron. "It's a long distance. Could you fly us there?"

Zenisa interrupted. "Could you fly there? Yes. Could you land there? No. There is a powerful spell shielding much of Solisa's lands.
"

"On foot it is." Gage stood. "We need to get started if we are going to reach her before she begins wielding the spell."

Suleima remained seated. "Will you help us against your sister?"

Zenisa hesitated.

"That's answer enough." Suleima rose to her feet. "Will you at least tell us what resources she has at her disposal?"

"She has spies all over her territory. You will not find it easy to get to her. Fae creatures of all kinds have sworn their allegiance to her and will defend her to the death. You should not risk yourselves to face her there."

"Where do you propose we face her? Because whether we die stopping her from performing the spells in the book, or because of the spells in that book, we are dead anyway. The promise of death has been on my horizon most of the last few years. I'd rather die fighting to save others than cower in hiding while innocents lose their lives to a tyrant. It didn't stop me against Dirrin or Kylin—"

"They are nothing compared to Solisa!" Zenisa interrupted viciously.

"Solisa may be more powerful than they were, but her ideals are just as heinous. I won't stand by and quietly wait for my death. At the very least, I'll take her with me."

Turning on her heel, Suleima walked to the door, Gage and Agron on her heels.

Dynasira's voice still reached her ears as she approached the door. "Zia would have stood with us. Solisa may be your sister, but she cannot be allowed to use that book. You can hide up here in your ice cave, but she will eventually be on your doorstep if we can't stop her. Will she hesitate to end you?"

Once out of Zenisa's home, back onto the snow- and ice-covered ground, Gage communicated with Kaly, updating her. "It'll be safer in the long run if we keep our group small. I think stealth will be more important than force in this case."

Dynasira and Agron shifted, flying them to the edge of the Sun Goddess's territory before landing. They camped for a night and left as the sun rose, starting the long trek to the heart of Solisa's land.

Chapter 19

THIS PART OF THE Sun Goddess's territory claimed mild temperatures and an abundance of vegetation. Trees reached high into the sky full of bright green leaves and the songs of numerous species of birds.

Suleima reached out periodically with her senses to keep tabs on any dangers. They stuck to the trees as they walked, keeping behind cover. Despite the mild temperatures, the uneven terrain and anxiety caused sweat to roll off her. Suleima stopped to pack away her jacket before picking up her bow again and continuing.

Movement in the corner of her eye drew her attention, but Suleima didn't see anything. No one else noticed and she couldn't sense anything, so they continued along their jagged path, staying within the cover of the trees.

Hours later, they sat down to have some lunch with the crackers, jerky and dried berries they carried with them. Koa did his best to provide comic relief as he darted from person to person, snatching berries and sipping from their canteens.

"You haven't seen or smelled anything?" Suleima asked.

"Not a thing." Gage adjusted his angle a bit so he could look at her and still watch their surroundings.

"Us either," Agron added.

"I wish we could fly here." Dynasirsa shuddered. "Or even drive. It would make this much faster."

Gage was quiet for a minute, staring off into the trees then said, "Kaly reports that it has been quiet near the caverns and the jinn since we left. They are still trying to release Hamanad without the book, but no luck so far. He seems to be stable as he is though."

Suleima nodded, and stood, Koa nestling into her shoulder, tired after his antics. As she turned to head out again, the movement was back. She pointed into the distance. "None of you saw that?"

They hadn't.

Suleima stepped forward, only to smack into a tree. She stumbled backward.

"Better watch where you're going," Agron chimed in, humor lacing his tone.

"It wasn't there a moment ago."

Three sets of furrowed brows regarded her.

"Yes, it was." Dynasira argued.

"Do you need to rest a bit longer?" Gage asked, searching her face.

"No," she deadpanned, turned on her heel and stepped around the tree which *hadn't* been there a minute before.

The sound of running water accompanied them throughout the day. "The river we keep hearing, which side of us was it on when we started out?"

"The left," Gage answered, understanding dawning on his face. "But it was on the right when we stopped for lunch and now it is to the south. But we've never crossed it."

Suleima trotted off toward the sound of the river, having to consciously switch directions three times before it finally came into view.

The crystalline surface sparkled with the pinks and oranges in the fading light of the sunset, enormous fish gliding in the waters below, some bobbing to the surface to grab a tasty insect. The inlet of the river was visible about a mile away where the ocean met the land at the junction of the border of Solisa's land.

They had barely traveled a mile after walking the entire day.

The damn trees were herding them, keeping them from making any progress. The canopy was too dense to use the sun for direction.

A mirthless laugh escaped. It was either that or cry. "Let's camp here tonight. We will follow the river tomorrow and hope it doesn't take us in circles too. Walking around blindly in the dark is a worse option than camping in the open at this point."

Suleima lay awake for hours, the weight of the situation and the frustration of the day staying in the forefront of her mind. So many people were counting on her. It seemed each of the challenges thrown at her these last years were growing in threat. She fumbled through the battles with Dirrin, felt inept the entirety of the struggles with Kylin and learning to use her fae magic, and now, Solisa. All of these magic-wielders, and they all had an affinity for fire. She rubbed her hand over the burn scars covering her left arm. Though hidden from sight with her glamor, the texture of the hard, scarred ridges could still be felt. Despite the mild temperatures, a chill stole over her body at the thought of facing fire once more. Her mentor, Erist, always tried to impress upon her the importance of being able to use each of the magic affinities, whether it was a dominant power or a minor one. She'd seen firsthand the destruction of water, wind, and earth. But fire scared her for as long as she could remember.

Gage rolled over and drew her into him. "Sleep. We will need to keep watch soon. Sleep while you can."

"She's so much more powerful than anything I have ever faced before."

"You won't face her alone."

Suleima wiggled out of his arms and sat up. "I can't sleep. Dynasira might as well get some rest." She was grateful he didn't protest her abrupt departure as she walked to where Dynasira stood, watching the horizon. "Go rest."

Dynasira watched her closely, then sat down, stretching out to lay at Suleima's feet. "If you are thinking of leaving us behind because it will be dangerous for us, you better think again."

"I'm not. I won't, Dyna," Suleima promised. "I've not been able to sleep. I might as well let you get rest."

"I'll rest fine right here."

Suleima shook her head. "I'm not stupid enough to think I can take on Solisa alone. The four of us may not even be a match for her. Me by myself? Not a chance."

Dynasira lifted up to her elbow. "You've always doubted your ability to handle whatever this crazy life has thrown at you. And yet, every time, you've walked away. You need to stop underestimating yourself."

"I don't remember it, but I know for a fact, you carried me from that first battlefield so long ago."

Dynasira waved her hand dismissively and lay back down. "Details. You're the one still left to fight, while he is a pile of ash, scattered to the winds. No one expects you to do it on your own."

"Solisa isn't Dirrin."

"Nope. I didn't think it was possible, but somehow she is cockier than he was. That will be her downfall." Dynasira closed her eyes, and her breathing evened out, sound asleep within moments.

Suleima envied her friend's ability to take things so nonchalantly. She wanted to be Dynasira when she grew up.

Walking closer to the river's edge, Suleima watched the horizon, her head on a swivel as she lowered her hand into the current of the river. A tingling sensation rushed over her hand, and she pulled it from the water. The water clung to her, a second skin that crept up her arm. She shook her hand to dislodge it.

Her panic must have leaked over the bond because Gage stirred, leaping to his feet and coming straight for.

The water crept higher and higher, soaking her sleeve.

An electric buzz against her skin zapped toward Gage when he tried to touch her arm.

Dynasira and Agron joined them a moment later.

Suleima flexed her right hand, the water moving with her. Cool to the touch, the water shimmered as it would if she had pulled it into a shield. Cautiously, she touched her right hand to her left. The water hissed at the contact, retreating an instant, then glomming onto her left hand, spreading up her other arm as well.

She held up her hand in front of her face, tilting it this way and that, inspecting the curious behavior of the water. It didn't feel like she was doing anything to cause the water to behave this way.

Reaching the top of both arms, the water stopped progressing but didn't dissipate either. Suleima took a few calming breaths. She closed her eyes and visualized what she wanted to happen, gliding the water with her fae magic away from her arms, but it refused to obey, fighting against her. Suleima tried pushing at it with her shamanistic magic, but again it resisted, clinging harder, almost painfully, to her skin as it fought against her magic.

Gage tentatively reached out to her again, only to be shoved back by another current of electricity. He growled in response and moved back in at the same time as Dynasira. Each were rewarded once again with another jolt.

"What is happening?" Dynasira asked.

Suleima started to shrug, when she felt it. She halted her movement and laughed. Reaching her hand up to her shoulder, she pulled Koa from where he hid under the edge of her shirt collar.

He bounced into her hand and splashed at the thin veil of water covering her, waving his vine-like arms into the air, his feet spreading like roots to keep him from tumbling off.

"Did you discover a new trick, Koa?" Suleima asked.

His cheerful chirps answered her before the water began to retreat, pooling into the hand holding Koa. His roots absorbed the water, and he grew an inch right before her eyes. The rest of the water covering her retreated.

"Did The Green Knight have power over water?" Dynasira asked.

"Not to my knowledge."

"Then how can he do that?" Dynasira eyed him warily.

"Again, I don't know," Suleima answered. "Maybe because of the magic Zenisa was using when he was created?"

"Or is he siphoning off of you?" The growl in Gage's voice plainly indicated what he thought of that scenario.

Koa blew raspberries at Gage before skittering up Suleima's arm and hiding under her hair.

Chapter 20

"WE'LL KEEP THE RIVER in view today," Suleima said, throwing her pack over her shoulder and lifting her bow. The sunrise's bold orange and reds faded, a bright blue sky covering them as they headed along the river into Solisa's territory. "Let's hope we get more than a mile."

Keeping the river in sight, they walked to the edge of the tree line to keep some cover, emerging out of cover anytime the river veered off. No one spoke, everyone listening for any sign of danger.

The others eyed Koa warily after the incident with the water the night before, but Suleima trusted her gut and it said Koa was harmless to her.

Their next section to travel was difficult. While the river stayed in sight, it got further and further away as they climbed along a cliff face. The increasingly difficult terrain had them sweating and out of breath. Suleima was forced to sling her bow over her shoulder and use both hands to keep her from tumbling down the wicked paths they traversed.

The treacherous terrain left them with no choice but to stop on the narrow and treacherous path, Suleima conjured a flame and encased it in an orb of air, a makeshift flashlight to light their way until they could reach an area wide enough to camp safely. Once again, she marveled at the ease with which she pulled fire. It came eagerly to her call and produced a light brighter than she'd ever conjured before.

By the time the ground leveled out enough for them to set up camp to rest for a bit, dawn peeked over the horizon. Exhausted wasn't strong enough of a word to cover how Suleima was feeling, and by the looks of the others, they were in just as bad of shape. Like zombies, they stumbled through setting up camp. She left Koa near her bag and gathered firewood. Suleima trudged along the edge of the wooded area just out of sight of the river, her mind cloudy with fatigue, stumbling several times.

She realized, too late, it had been too long since she scanned the area for a threat. A heavy weight slammed into her back, ramming her to the ground and pinning her there. Suleima landed hard on the pile of firewood in her arms, knocking the wind out of her and cutting off her startled cry of pain.

Not that she could use it from the ground, but her bowstring was caught between her, the firewood, and the ground. Both hands were pinned beneath her and the weight holding her there twisted back and forth, driving her further into the dirt.

The thing on her back grabbed her braid and yanked her head back, straining her neck and making it even more difficult for her to make any kind of noise. With the pressure at the center of her back, she was unable to squirm loose and the assailant stood at her side, making her attempts at kicking futile. It leaned down. Its hot, foul breath assaulted her as it wafted to her nose from behind. The creature snarled as a drip ran from the back of her neck, over Gage's bite mark and down her chest. The slimy texture of its drool caused a shudder to run through her body.

She wanted to scream. She wanted to vomit. But most of all, her anger surged, and she wanted to fight. Suleima fought against its superior strength, rocking her weight back and forth, trying to free her hands. She concentrated on the earth around her, pushing it to give more wiggle room. A hairy fist slammed down next to her face and she stilled. Her left hand was nearly free. Its inferior strength, grip, and sense of touch meant she'd do less damage, but she wouldn't go down without a fight.

Still grinding her into the ground with its weight, it didn't seem to be trying to kill her only hold her. For what? She didn't know, but had no desire to stick around and find out.

The creature stood to her right, so Suleima continued to wiggle and squirm until her left hand was freed, then shifted her weight quickly, bringing up her left knee so she could reach the knife she kept there. Grabbing the knife, she swung her left hand in a high arc and embedded the knife into the thigh of the creature.

It let out a horrifying bellow and momentarily lifted the weight from her back.

Suleima took advantage of it and rolled away from the beast and up onto her feet. She looked up and up and up. The creature had to be nine feet tall. A thick gold loop through the septum of its wide nose. It snorted heavily and stomped its hoof, her knife not sticking out of its thigh like she thought, but out of the side of its hock joint. The minotaur's shaggy mane shifted menacingly as it bellowed once again, then lowered its massive head, aiming to spear her with its horns.

She let it charge at her, tucking and rolling out of its path, and ripping her knife out of its knee as it barreled past, unable to stop its momentum.

The minotaur caught its shoulder on a tree before its hooves found enough purchase to stop, then spun back to face her. The next bellow was nearly drowned out by the howl of Gage's wolf as he rushed into the scene, Dynasira and Agron not far behind. And then she noticed three new minotaurs emerging from the trees behind the first.

"Looks like you found more than firewood, Sul," Dynasira said dryly, stepping to the side a few paces, making room for Agron and herself to shift.

"Decided to make some new friends," she answered, adjusting her grip on the knife now in her right hand. "The first one is injured, but not badly. He took a knife to the knee after pinning me in the dirt."

Gage's eyes blazed and his hackles rose even further. He positioned himself between her and the minotaurs, but she stepped up to his shoulder.

"I'm not done here," Suleima said, taking up a fighting stance. The knife handle, smooth in her palm, offered comfort as she faced off with her friends at her side. They were too close for her to get a shot off with the bow. The knife would have to do.

Dynasira shifted and roared, her enormous blue wings spreading out, making her look much larger. The minotaur closest to her retreated a few steps at the sight.

Agron was next, his posturing causing another minotaur to shrink back.

The two facing her and Gage stood their ground. They stomped their hooves in unison. Whatever signal it was, it brought the other two back into line and they all stomped together, snorting and bellowing. A thundering sound came from every direction it seemed.

Suleima pulled at the earth beneath their feet, only to have all four sets of the minotaurs' eyes lock onto her, scorching with rage and intensity. In unison, their fists slammed into the ground, halting the pull of her magic, just as the first one had done when she was still pinned. The minotaur must be tied to fae earth magic, so she gripped the knife tighter as the first minotaur stepped forward.

The others followed suit, stepping as one. They lowered their heads and charged aiming to impale.

Gage danced out of the way, snagging one in the hock and tearing away flesh. Each of them stumbled.

Suleima slashed with her knife as she spun away from her minotaur, slicing a deep gash in its thick shoulder. The other three minotaurs dropped their shoulders on the same side as the one she injured.

Dynasira grabbed the one closest to her, lifted it with her talon and tossed it into the others, bowling them over, legs tangling and arms flailing every which way.

The cacophony of bellowing and snorting continued, as they fought to untangle themselves, gnashing their huge, flat cow-like teeth at each other.

Suleima backed into the center of the dragons with Gage at her side. "Solisa has altered them somehow. There's no intelligence, no speech. And, when we hurt one of them, it effects the rest."

Suleima pulled with fire. Her pack with her supplies remained at the camp, but even at this distance, her fingers tingled with the fire the others started while she searched for wood. She pushed the spark, blasting it against the tree directly behind the minotaurs' flailing bodies, exploding it into a burst of fireworks. A thick branch splintered off and fell onto them, further hampering their ability to recover. The creatures bellowed in fear, their eyes rolling wildly, their movements frantic.

The minotaurs regained their feet. One tried to stomp, but it knocked itself and the others off balance.

Gage turned sharply to her and growled, probably seeing her plan in his head from their bond.

Suleima pulled a shield over her and ran into the middle of the group of minotaurs. They roared and raised their fists on their uninjured arms, bringing them down in vicious strikes, but without intelligent thought, their fists came down on each other. Sickening thuds could be heard through the shield she held as the bashing continued. Blood spurted, their balances waning as they swayed from the force of the blows they continued to land on each other as they tried to break through her shield.

Agron roared into the fray, unleashing his acid spray.

Gage howled, unable to reach her now because of the acid, his anger and impatience bleeding through the bond.

The minotaurs dropped to the ground as the acid, the last blow, seeped into the open wounds on their heads, finally ending their fight.

Dynasira spit water at her, clearing the acid from Suleima's shield and cleaning a path for her.

As the adrenaline dropped, the threat gone, Suleima felt the overwhelm of exhaustion overtake her and stumbled, only to be lifted into Gage's arms and carried back to camp.

He shushed her when she tried to protest. "Dyna and Agron will take care of the rest. You and I can't touch his acid. You'll rest where I can keep an eye on you. No more firewood for you."

When she woke next, the sun was high in the sky, Gage's wolf was her pillow, resting but with his ears perked, listening, as he had done so many times on Mount Lucent. Dynasira and Agron rested a few feet away. Suleima rolled to her feet and tried to stretch out some of the soreness.

Gage lifted one sleepy eyelid to watch her.

"I'm not venturing anywhere. I'll keep watch, you rest now." Suleima crouched by the fire and poked at the embers. She added some of the firewood Agron and Dynasira must have brought back after taking care of the minotaurs. Suleima gave a slight tug with her fire magic and coaxed the flames, igniting the fresh fuel. She walked a few more paces and knelt beside the river, her fingers tingling as the water rushed over them.

She relaxed herself, opening her senses to be alerted to anything unusual, but allowed her vision to unfocus, mulling over the events of the day before. The minotaurs acted strangely, almost as if they were the same. When one was hurt, the others displayed the same weakness. Zenisa had said Solisa liked to experiment with creatures, to diminish their weaknesses, like she had with the nuckelavees, making them no longer weak to fresh water, along with the creation of Kylin, a former shaman, making her an energy vampire. Suleima didn't know much about minotaurs, other than their appearance. However, she couldn't see any benefit to nature by making the injury of one affect the others. It had to be some sort of unnatural mutation.

Her vision sharpened as a thought popped into her head.

Dirrin altered the banshees to make them corporeal at times. They could shift back and forth, giving them the ability to harm others physically as well as with their wails. That was the connection with him and Solisa. He had the book, found it for her. He was gathering power to prepare for the spells. When he failed, Solisa sent Kylin next. But, why use them as pawns?

Tests. Dirrin and Kylin must have been tests to see what sort of resistance she would find. And when Suleima and her friends managed to stop both of them—that's why she was back in her territory and not out casting the spells now. She's prepping reinforcements to keep them from stopping her.

They needed to reach her and retrieve the book and key before Solisa finished preparing. Catching her off guard would be their only hope. She had access to much more power than either Dirrin or Kylin.

Only a few hours of daylight remained when Dynasira joined her, still on the edge of the river. "Are we staying here tonight or traveling through the night?"

"We need to find Solisa as soon as possible. But, we also need to be rested. It is going to be a fine line keeping that balance."

Gage approached and sat behind her, resting his chin on her shoulder, his arms wrapping around her. "There's a full moon tonight. If we stay near the river and out of the trees, we can hike for a few hours. A short rest should be enough, then we can get moving again at dawn."

Suleima nodded, leaning into the warmth he provided, contrasting the chill of the water.

"I'll get some food going," Dynasira said.

Gage turned Suleima to face him, examining her face closely.

"I'm ok. I'm rested." Suleima smiled at him.

Finding whatever evidence he needed in her face, he drew her lips to his. "I worry about the toll this is all taking on you," he said as he ended the kiss.

"After this is all said and done, I'm not going to lie, I'm going to sleep for a week and not leave my woods."

"As long as I can come too."

"Always." Suleima cuddled into his arms for another minute, absorbing his strength and warmth. All too soon, they would be on their way again, heading straight into danger.

Chapter 21

THEY HIKED ALONG THE river's edge, foraging for plants and hunting small animals at the edge of the woods to save some of their rations. Crankiness ran rampant among them, the tension building as they waited for the next attack, the next challenge.

It wasn't until dusk on the second day that they encountered another creature. The deafening roar set Suleima on alert and had Gage shifting. She pulled her bow and nocked an arrow as they stopped, waiting for the creature to emerge from the tree line.

A large being stood on the edge of her senses. It was too far for her to determine the species. For the sound of its roar to travel that far, and be so loud, she didn't think seeking out the creature would be a smart decision.

Suleima motioned for them to continue, but no one dropped their guard as they walked. Gage prowled back and forth, getting ahead of them for a bit before backtracking. Uneasiness threatened to choke Suleima when he got too close to the woods, but he'd hurry back to her side. The presence never left, right at the edge of her perception, an ever-present threat, skyrocketing the tension trying to consume them.

The river began to curl into the forest, the tree line splitting to allow its passage. Suleima stopped and set down her pack, her bow still in hand. "That creature is still out there. It's getting dark and, within the trees, the light will be worse. We'll camp here tonight and enter the woods at dawn."

Dynasira and Agron ate quickly, then shifted into their dragon forms to rest and keep watch through the night. Suleima set up her usual wards and refilled her power wells before crawling into her sleeping bag beside an already snoozing Koa and Gage, still pacing in his wolf form. Suleima patted the space next to her, hoping he would rest. He laid down at the top of her sleeping bag, acting as her protector and pillow as she drifted off.

Gage's low growl woke her. It seemed as if she had only slept a few minutes, but the light peeking up on the horizon indicated morning arrived. She followed his gaze to the edge of the woods.

Agron was on his feet, wings spread, making him appear larger than he was. She couldn't see Dynasira, but just beyond Agron stood a troll.

At least eleven feet tall, probably more, the green and brown mottled skin sprouted tufts of hair in random spots. His mouth gaped, exposing sharply pointed, gray and green teeth in the front and flattened, grinding teeth in the rear. Yellowish drool dripped from his chin and he wore a skirt of leather and leaves. Enormously muscled arms hung down, hands in line with his knees. A club dragged on the ground from one hand. The muscles of its arm bunched and rippled as it heaved the heavy club up to rest on its shoulder and sneered. If he'd only had one eye, he'd have been a twin to a cyclops.

Suleima climbed to her feet, bow in hand.

The troll narrowed its bulging, yellow-tinged eyes and tightened its grip on the club. The light from the rising sun was blocked by thick clouds.

Like a soft breath, magic drifted over and around her, exploring—what it was looking for, she didn't know. Suleima pulled up a shield of magic around her, blocking the exploration.

The troll huffed and stomped its foot.

Suleima backed up a step, her stance more defensive. "He's got magic," she said loud enough for Dynasira to hear. "He shouldn't have it, but he does."

Hackles raised, Gage let out a vicious growl, putting himself between Suleima and the troll.

The troll slammed his club onto the ground. The reverberation rumbled through Suleima's knees.

Dynasira sprayed him from behind with boiling water at the same time Suleima loosed an arrow.

Gage ran at him, harrying him with bites to his calves.

The troll kicked out with his feet, narrowly missing Gage.

Agron's angry roar had Suleima spinning on the spot. Surrounded by a net, Agron flailed and bit at the offending structure. The net dragged at him, pulling him closer to the river.

Suleima pulled her knife as she ran toward the livid, green dragon writhing in the net. She was blasted backward as her hand connected with the ropes—ropes of magic. *What the hell is Solisa doing to these creatures?*

Only ten or so feet from the bank of the river now, Agron's claws left deep gouges in the earth where his talons tried to find purchase.

Suleima pulled at her earth magic and sunk Agron's talons into the dirt, solidifying it. It worked to slow his progress toward the river, but the net continued to yank him toward the river, hauling him onto his back, his legs bending at a painful angle.

Agron's next roar was a mix of frustration and pain.

Suleima released his legs from the earth and grabbed her pack, reaching deep into its depths, as she pulled water from the river and air from around her. She bent the water, molding it with the air to create a bubble around Agron as his feet left the bank and he plunged into the rushing river.

She dove in after him, using her fae magic to ease the river's speed and strength. Her hand wrapped in the fae cloth from her pack, Suleima closed her fist over the thickest of the ropes holding Agron. She felt the buzzing of a thousand angry bees beneath the cloth, but it couldn't blast her back, this time.

Agron struggled against the ropes, but had air to breathe, thanks to her bubble.

Suleima placed the blade of her knife on the rope, only to have it melt on contact. Kicking to the surface, she gasped in her own breath before diving back down. She heaved with her earth magic, dragging a large boulder onto the base of the net, preventing the slowed current from dragging Agron any further down the river. Suleima glanced around, trying to figure out how to get rid of the net. Nothing jumped out at her as helpful and her mind raced as panic began to set in.

Gage's worry for her bled through their bond, as well as his anger. His fight with the troll flashing in her mind, showed him uninjured, but still brawling alongside Dynasira.

She surfaced again, gulped more air, and dove down, using her fae magic to speed her descent.

The bubble around Agron shrunk as he breathed in the resource. She pulled some air, shoving more into the bubble. The action sparked an idea. She quickly fed more air in before turning her attention to the ropes. Suleima fed fae magically charged water into the ropes of the net, working quickly, rolling wave after wave of water into the strands of the rope. With each wave of water, the magicked fibers of the rope separated further apart. She was running low on air herself but didn't dare stop. Sparkles appeared in her vision as the last of the fibers separated enough for Agron, shifted down to his human size, to slip through.

Panting hard as she surfaced, Suleima slapped at the water as she desperately tried to make it to shore. The battle with the troll was still raging on and she felt pain through the bond where Gage must have been hit by the troll along his flank.

Agron's talon, emerging from the water as he shifted back, closed over her and lifted Suleima out of the water, setting her down on the edge of the shore before diving in to help Gage and Dynasira. She coughed up river water as she staggered to her feet and stumbled toward the raging brawl. She pulled at earth feeling it ripple out from her, gathering momentum, the ground undulating beneath the feet of the troll, knocking him off balance.

His club swung in a wide arc, like a professional golfer, aimed at Gage's ribs.

Suleima jammed her hand in the earth; a hand of dirt emerging from behind Gage. She grabbed his tail, yanking him out of the way at the last possible second. She reached into the fire and grabbed a half-lit log, hurling it at the troll, sending a spark of fire and air at the log as it reached the troll's face, exploding the log and momentarily blinding the troll.

The troll spun away from the flames, exposing his bright red back to her. Blisters had formed on his skin from the scalding water Dynasira had spit at him. Dynasira hit him square in the face with another blast as his painful shriek blasted the air.

Gage pinned his ears back at the sound. Agron clipped the troll's shoulder with his wing, further upsetting his balance.

When the troll hit his knees, Suleima loosed another arrow, this one piercing his neck. Gage danced out of the way of spurting blood and made his way over toward her, shifting and checking her for injuries.

"I'm ok," she assured him as Dynasira and Agron joined them.

"Has Solisa been altering these creatures for a long time? Or is this an effort to stall us, or keep us distracted?" Agron asked.

"I'd say she's likely been doing this for a while. I believe Dirrin learned from her. Them stalling us is just a bonus."

"You used a lot of magic back there," Gage observed.

"I'll rest later. We need to get moving," Suleima replied, already gathering her pack, bow, and Koa.

Gage's hand on her arm stalled her movements. "We have time."

"I don't want to stay with the troll's body." She cast her eyes downward and swallowed hard. The image of the troll with her arrow in its neck haunted her. She may have had to kill so many creatures over the last few years, but it would never get easier.

Gage waved Dynasira and Agron on before tilting her chin up so their eyes met. "You've done nothing wrong."

A tear slipped past her tight control and left a trail down her cheek. "I shouldn't be leading this. I'll never get used to this feeling after taking a life."

"That's exactly why you *should* be leading this." Gage gathered her in his arms and held her tightly against him, careful to keep her turned away from the sight of the fallen troll.

Chapter 22

A FEELING OF DREAD hovered over her. The darkness as the sun inched closer to the horizon mirrored her mood. They'd already stopped for her to rest and recharge, which added more time to their already long journey. Suleima wanted to get to Solisa as quickly as possible, but each step was a struggle as her mind warred over the necessity of the confrontation and her dread of the deaths that would inevitably follow. Gage hovered nearby, giving her space, allowing her to stand on her own, but never far away, a constant source of support.

They trudged through the heavily forested area, noticing little homes nestled among the trees, Suleima slowed their pace, and they made sure to keep out of sight.

The little homes were dilapidated, hastily thrown together. Cheerful flower boxes dotted some of the homes, an attempt to make them homier. Large gallows were constructed in clearings within full view of the homes, some had remains still hanging from them, mostly decayed and skeletal. Demonstrating how poorly Solisa's subjects were treated and the scare tactics used against them, a guillotine, the blade still smeared with old blood, sat in the center of a group of houses.

At one such small village, Suleima froze as a familiar enormous hat came into view. Looking much the same as he had when they'd seen him, the nuberu swung from his neck in the town center. The ghastly sight weakened her knees, causing her to stumble. Only Gage's hand on her arm kept her from running out of the trees, and into the clearing where he hung. Even from this distance, visible burns marred the nuberu's mottled skin. More bruises and burns could be seen through the many tears on his clothing and a horrifying grimace would forever remain frozen on the poor creature's face.

He may have attacked them, but no one deserved to be tortured. But, when she took her eyes off the nuberu, she spotted an even more disturbing sight. Lined up next to him, in much the same condition were what must be his two children and two adults.

So engrossed with the horror she faced, Suleima failed to notice Dynasira's disappearance, until she suddenly reappeared with a piece of parchment crushed in her hands. She held it out to Suleima, but it was Gage who took it and opened it.

Attention Subjects:

Failure to accomplish tasks set forth by your Goddess will result in, not only the severe punishment and death of the failure, but of those who are responsible for the creation of the failure, its spouse, and all its offspring

A few feet away, the body of another small person swung in the wind. Was it a child? A small fae like the symbriole? There wasn't enough of it left to tell.

Gage laid a calming hand on the back of her neck as they crept from tree to tree. Until that moment, she hadn't realized how tense her body had become, her hands clenched, her teeth grinding. He stopped her behind a thick tree and took both of her hands in his. Taking deep, calming breaths, he rested his forehead on hers and encouraged her to breathe with him. His voice was barely a whisper when he said, "I feel your tension, your anger. We will work to change it, but we can't change it from here."

Suleima closed her eyes, leaning into him and steadying her breathing. She consciously loosened her muscles and unclenched her jaw, welcoming the calmness he provided, absorbing the peace. "Those bodies... The cruelty..."

Gage pulled her tighter, enveloping her in his arms. "There's nothing we can do about it here and now. We need to find Solisa."

She let him take her weight, take her burden, for a moment before steeling her knees and nodding. She wound her fingers through his and stepped away from the tree, refusing to drop his hand, needing his strength to get her through.

The sadness of the small villages they passed sunk into her bones. Despair and desperation hung over the homes like a cloud. She clung tighter to Gage's hand, suppressing her need to approach the homes and the people within. She needed to assist them in any way she could—listen to their stories, heal wounds, provide food and water.

When they approached a clearing late in the day, about an hour's walk from the last village, Suleima slumped against a tree. Exhaustion dragged at her, not from fighting or working magic, but the soul-deep exhaustion of hopelessness.

Dynasira and Agron eyed her, concern written on their features, but she was too weary to reassure them.

Gage murmured, too low for her to hear, and they walked off into the trees. Gage turned on his heel and came to her side, lifting her into his arms, after setting Koa down on her pack. He walked to the edge of the river and sat down, her in his lap.

She buried her face in his neck, holding on for dear life. She was too sad to cry. One hand held her to him, while the other worked off her boots and socks. The icy water skimmed over her toes. She dropped one hand from around his neck, still clinging to him with the other, and buried it in the dirt and rocks they sat on. Taking in a lungful of air, she connected back to the elements, pulling them around her like a blanket. She lifted her eyes to his and saw the fire burning there. The spark. His connection to fire through Volos, the first of his kind. Her connection to him through their bond, and the fire he ignited within her. Their lips met in a frenzy. She needed to forget, to be surrounded by nothing but him, to ignore the outside world, if only for a moment.

All too soon, Dynasira cleared her throat, alerting them that she and Agron had returned, their arms laden with firewood.

This time, when she wrapped her arm around him, his peace and calm grounded her as she dropped her head to his shoulder, taking in the serene views around them. Surrounded by his scent, his strength, she tried to push away, even for a moment, the horrors she was about to face. For once, she would allow Dynasira and Agron to set up camp. They were here to help her and she could let them do more than help keep watch and fight when the need arose. It was finally sinking in; she wasn't alone in this.

As the sun peeked over the horizon, Suleima stood reveling in the feel of the cool morning breeze caressing her cheeks. Koa toddled over and tugged lightly at her pants as he climbed. When she lifted him to her shoulder, he snuggled right into her neck.

Koa patted her neck and chirped, pointing to the river.

Suleima knelt beside the rushing waters, dunking her hand in.

As before, the water clung to her skin, slowly seeping up her arm, teasing at Koa's feet on her shoulder like waves on the shoreline. She felt less panic now, understanding from this was Koa's doing. Touching her left hand to her right, the water continued to spread up her other arm. The scar tissue muted the sensation of the cool liquid on her left arm, but she followed it with her eyes.

Koa climbed to the front of her neck, clinging to the top of her shirt collar, hanging like a miniature rock climber. Tendrils snaked out from his arms, teasing at the water on each of her shoulders until the waters met at her neck.

Panic began to rise, stealing her breath. Water lifted in a pulse, licking at her chin with each wave and the coolness drifted down over her chest and torso as the water spread down. She gulped at the air, but the water never reached past her chin, the movement of the waves continuing, but not advancing. She took a calming breath as her anxiety subsided with the realization.

"Sul?" Gage said from a few feet behind her. Worry for her bled through their bond.

She turned away from the river to look at him. "It's okay. I'm okay."

He cautiously reached out to touch her again but yanked his hand away as soon as the electric pulse zapped hungrily at him.

An idea sparked.

"Gage, open my pack and grab the fae cloth," she instructed. When he did as she asked and returned, she continued, "Wrap it completely around your hand, then reach out to me again."

He did as she instructed and covered his hand. He hesitated a moment but reached out and wrapped his fingers around her forearm. "There's aggressive buzzing under the cloth. I can feel that, but it's not throwing me back like before."

"That's what I felt with the troll's ropes trapping Agron. Can I try something?"

At Gage's nod, she reached out and touched his arm, above the edge of the cloth on his bare skin.

"There's still a buzzing sensation, but it's not shocking me like before."

Dynasira reached out to her other side, but stepped back quickly, shaking the hand she used. "So it's a shield of some kind?"

Suleima looked down at Koa, now standing on her forearm above Gage's hand, splashing and dancing in the film of water undulating over her arms and torso. She laughed at his antics, then picking him up she looked at his leaf-covered face, his little black eyes blinking as he squeaked and chirped at her. "Can you help me drop this shield?"

This time Suleima reached out with her senses and followed Koa's movements closely as the water receded from her body and arms. She concentrated on the magic and danced her hands along, following the rhythm she sensed.

When the last of the magic faded, she placed Koa into Gage's palm and knelt beside the river, plunging her hand back into the water. Using the magic as she'd felt it from Koa, Suleima glided her fae magic against her skin, watching as the shimmering film of water crept up her arm to her elbow. It moved much slower than Koa managed, but she'd done it.

When she couldn't coax it any further, she watched as the water slowly receded before the last of the water dropped to the ground. "That will take more practice," Suleima said, turning back to her friends who were watching her closely. "Thank you, Koa, for showing me."

She retrieved Koa from Gage and walked him over, beyond the campfire, setting him on the ground and giving him some fresh soil and water to play and rest in. Suleima turned back to her friends and chose a stump around the fire to sit on. Looking up as Gage hauled his log closer to hers, Dynasira and Agron took their places across the fire. "So the water is a fae shield of sorts. It may be a better shield than the one I can make using both my magics, but I can't know for sure until I test it."

Dynasira gave her a skeptical look. "What do you mean by 'test it?'"

"I'll try to test it against fire first. Regular and magical fire. If it holds, I'll try it with your water and Agron's acid."

"No!" Gage and Dynasira roared together.

Suleima raised her hand to stop their protest. "Would you rather I test it in the middle of facing Solisa?"

His low growl told her that he knew she was right, but he wasn't happy about it.

Chapter 23

As LIGHT DAWNED THE next morning, Suleima sat back at the campfire, watching Dynasira rekindle the fire without any magical influence. Before long, a cheerful fire crackled and spit, the sparks dancing through the smoke as they drifted into the air, winking out a few feet above the fire. Gage paced, his hands flexing and tightening. He'd tried to talk her out of this several times last night and this morning. He understood it was a necessary risk, but he didn't like the idea of putting her in that position.

Suleima stood and went to him, stopping in front of him. She placed her hands on either side of his face and pulled his forehead to hers. As was becoming habit, she paused a moment, taking in his scent with long deep breaths. "I need to do this, and you need to let me."

He closed his eyes, the frustration threatening to boil over seeped through their bond.

"Do you need to take a walk?"

His eyes shot open, the fire in them made her smile. The growl had her giggling.

"Then, I need you to calm down. I will be careful," she assured him.

Dynasira caught her eye over Gage's shoulder. Suleima dropped a kiss to the end of his nose and gave him a hug before stepping around him and walking to the riverbank, Gage shadowing her the whole way.

She knelt next to the water and plunged her hand in. The chill raised goosebumps on her arms. Lifting her arm, the water quickly warmed to a more comfortable temperature and began its slow creep, enveloping her skin and lapping up her arm at a steady pace.

As the water neared her shoulder, Suleima touched her left hand to her right. She couldn't get the water to encase her torso as Koa had, but getting it to her shoulders was an improvement. She decided it would have to be enough for the test and turned, walking to the campfire.

Gage stayed at her hip as she reached into the fire and gripped a log. Lifting it from the fire, she felt nothing in her left hand, so she transferred it to her right. A slight warmth permeated the film of water on her skin. Inch by inch, she eased the lit end of the log closer and closer to her left hand. The water rippled and shimmered in response. The warmth increased enough that she could feel it through the scar tissue and nerve damage. When she touched the flames to the water, they sparked and sizzled. The heat increased, so she pulled her left hand away.

Gage was there in a moment, examining her hand for any damage. Suleima allowed him to look his fill. When he was satisfied, she traded hands with the log and repeated the process with her right hand. There was a marked difference in the warmth she felt with her right hand, but nothing she couldn't handle. She allowed Gage to repeat his inspection before she waved him away and shifted her focus.

The flames at the end of the log were gone, just sparking embers and heavy smoke after coming into contact with the water shimmering along her skin. Suleima pushed with air and yanked at the fire, the flames, white hot, erupting on the log, exploding the end and sending shards of burnt wood flying in different directions. Dynasira, Gage and Agron dove in different directions to avoid the shrapnel.

Much slower with the increased heat and magical properties of the fire on the remaining part of the log, Suleima inched it closer and closer to her right hand, until it sparked and sizzled once again at contact. The warmth was uncomfortable, but not hot enough to burn her. She pulled the fire from the log before tossing it back into their makeshift pit. Gage inspected her arm once again, and satisfied that she wasn't hurt, stepped back.

Suleima pulled with water and air, molding it into a shield to cover her from the front, and raised her left arm to the side as Dynasira shifted. Agron pulled Gage back and to the side a few steps to keep him out of range as Dynasira opened her jaw wide and spit out a stream of scalding water.

Again, she felt a slight warmth, and the pressure of the stream pushed her arm back, but there was no damage.

Agron was up next. He shifted and away from their camp and left a puddle of his acid.

Cautiously, Suleima approached and dipped the tip of her left pointer finger into the acid. There was an instant reaction. The water spit and trembled, attempting to remain in place, but the acid ate away at the water shield. She stepped over to the riverbank and immersed her left hand in the water, allowing the fast-moving water to wash away the acid before it hit her skin. When the area was clear of the acid, she released the magic holding the water to her skin and allowed it to drift back into the river.

"Note to self: don't expose the shield to Agron's poison."

Gage had her left hand in his, turning it over and over to find any hint of injury.

"I'm fine," she reassured him. "It ate away at the shield, but I washed it away before it could hurt me."

His arms wrapped around her, holding her and breathing in her scent.

She felt calmness seep into him, and in turn, into her.

When she stepped away from him, she took a seat, back on her log, near the fire. "We know now that the shield helps with regular and shamanistic fire, and scalding water from a dragon, but not acid. I'm hoping it will have at least some similar effect on fae fire. We can use as much defense against Solisa as possible."

They packed up camp and headed out for the day, again keeping to the river's edge.

Ahead of them, as the sun's last rays of the day began to fade, the river branched off into two forks. One turned further into the trees, while the other twisted and turned before heading in the opposite direction.

"Let's camp here and head into the trees at first light," Agron suggested.

"I'll grab some firewood," Dynasira said, setting down her pack. She paused halfway to standing, squinting at something in the river. She stepped to the side, and shifted, her royal blue eyes blazing as she spread her enormous blue wings. She arched and roared, the scales along her back clicking.

Beside her, Gage shifted and snarled, facing the water, the fur on his scruff standing on end as he scanned the river for whatever had caused Dynasira's reaction.

A series of black logs bobbed along the surface of the water. A second later, a large black balloon broke through the surface near the logs. White and sapphire blue eyes blinked open, the logs lifting from the water and slapping back down with a great crack. The angle of the sun's rays glinted off the black balloon revealing scattered blue dots that shimmered, glowing in the dimming light.

Suleima placed her hand on Gage's neck and smoothed down the fur there. "Easy Dyna," she said, her eyes never leaving the river's surface. "It's Urlanta."

The black tentacles swayed with the river's current as the symbriole worked her way to the shoreline. When she emerged from the water, she was back in her tiny cupid-like form with her extra-large, blinking, blue eyes focused on the massive blue dragon slightly behind Suleima. She tilted her head this way and that then took a step toward them.

Dynasira widened her wings and Agron stepped to the side, making room to shift as well.

Suleima held her hand up to stall them and stepped away from Gage. His low growl projected his warning, but he stayed where he was. When she was a few feet away, Suleima knelt at the symbriole's level. "What are you doing here?"

"Help." The symbriole's stilted speech was shaky and her eyes bounced from Dynasira's immense dragon to Gage to Agron, who was still ready to shift at a moment's notice, and back.

Keeping a wary eye on the others, Urlanta reached out her small, chubby hand and touched Suleima's cheek. Images swam in Suleima's mind—Solisa harming her symbriole pair, Solisa stealing the key, Suleima and the jinn helping to heal Urlanta's injury to her arm, and injuries after Solisa stole the key. "Help defeat Solisa."

Suleima sat back on her heels, losing contact with Urlanta. "We're resting for the night. We will turn into the trees at first light."

The symbriole nodded, then stepped closer to Suleima again. Slowly reaching out her hand again, she touched Suleima's cheek, causing her to freefall back into another vision.

Urlanta stood behind the same tree where Suleima had stared in horror at the bodies back in the village not long before.

The crack of a branch echoed like a gunshot, spinning Urlanta around to face the a small creature similar to Koa. A larger vine-like hand swept out from behind a tree, pulling the creature out of its eyeline, before it stepped out, it's chest puffed out to make it seem larger, more threatening.

"No harm," Urlanta said, stepping out from behind her own tree.

The creature tilted its head this way and that, closely examining Urlanta.

Urlanta took a small step forward and reached out to touch the creature's closest vine.

Suleima could see the vision Urlanta showed the creature, a highlight reel of Urlanta's encounters with Solisa, followed by her desire to end Solisa's cruelty.

The creature, seemingly a female, eyed Urlanta for another moment before speaking. "The Goddess sent the nuberu on a task. A task he originally refused." She swallowed hard and turned her head away from the sight of the bodies swinging. A tear tracked down her leafy face. "You should leave here. If the Goddess find you..."

Urlanta bowed her head. "Stay safe." She nodded from the creature to the child. "Both."

Urlanta's anger surged as the creatures disappeared back into the trees.

As the vision faded, the symbriole walked back to the edge of the river and tucked into a crevice, her wide eyes blinking and shifting, keeping watch.

Chapter 24

The hidden villages appeared more often, so they kept their voices down, only speaking when necessary. Urlanta stayed in the water, bobbing along in her kraken form, looking like logs floating in the current.

The thickness of the trees increased drastically the further they went, but they managed to keep the river in sight.

Her left palm itched. The left side of her face tingled. And, she felt a buzzing even through the canvas of her bag. The cloth was warning her again. Suleima stopped and took a deep breath. Gage, Dynasira, and Agron had all seen her scars before. She had nothing to fear. But still....

Gage retraced his steps, coming to a stop next to her and placing his hand on the small of her back, his presence radiating calm. "What's wrong?"

"I need to drop my glamor." The waiver in her voice betrayed her vulnerability. "I think if I use my magic, she'll know for certain that we are here."

"Then drop it. You don't need it." Gage shifted so he stood directly in front of her and bent down so their eyes aligned. "With or without the glamor, you are still you. Beautiful, inside and out."

The truth of his words blazed along their bond. His thumb wiped away a tear, her breath escaped in a shaky exhale, and her glamor fell away.

Gage dropped a kiss to her lips and laid his forehead on hers, breathing in her scent. "You've never needed your glamor for me." When she dropped her chin, he added, "You'll never need it."

It was mid-day when they emerged from the trees, and Urlanta climbed out of the river. The thundering of a waterfall was just ahead, the open meadow abruptly stopping on the edge of a cliff. Green grass in a range of shades stretched as far as the eye could see. Thick forests surrounded the immense meadow but looked like specks in the distance.

Sunlight glinted off a grand castle two-thirds of the distance between where they stood and the far edge of the forest. It was too far away to make out many details, but the red windows blazed in the light.

"There's no cover," Agron says, his eyes, like everyone else's, were transfixed on the castle. "No place to hide. We'll be easy pickings."

"Right now, we are no bigger than ants to anyone looking out of those windows. We can worry about that as we get closer," Suleima replied. Her mind spun with all the spells she could think of to use to help hide them, but her gut told her it would do more to call attention to them than the lack of cover. "For now, our strategy doesn't change.

We stay by the river once we get off this cliff. The river looks like it runs right up to the castle."

She led the charge to the edge of the cliff, peering over to see the several hundred-foot drop to the bottom.

Koa shivered on her shoulder, and she turned to him. She lifted him, staring into his tiny black eyes. "We won't let anything happen to you," she assured him. Suleima tucked him into her shirt pocket. Gage grabbed the waistband of her jeans as she leaned farther over the edge.

"Let's not tumble to our death today," his gruff voice betrayed his worry.

There appeared to be a ledge about halfway down and a narrow path leading downward from there, but no path led down from the top to it.

Suleima walked back to the bank of the rushing river. She paced back and forth, examining the speed of the water and the width of the river. Beckoning the others to follow, Suleima backtracked about half a mile, into the densest area of trees they passed that day. "I don't think I should use my magic within sight of the castle. My instincts are screaming that it would be a terrible idea. I need to see over the cliff on the other side of the river. I can't see past the waterfall, and while there is a ledge below, I can't see any way to get to it. This spot is the narrowest crossing we've seen today. Let's cross here and see what is below the other side."

Urlanta tugged at the bottom edge of Suleima's shirt to get her attention and raised her arm up. "Touch."

Suleima knelt and waited while the symbriole's hand laid gently on her cheek. The images flashed in Suleima's mind. Attacks from the red castle in the distance, *if* Suleima had used her magic within view of it, confirming her suspicions. Then, the images changed—Urlanta, in her kraken form, aiding each of them across the river without Suleima needing to use her magic, even here. "Thank you. We would greatly appreciate your help," she said, standing and explaining what she saw to the others.

Urlanta climbed back into the water, shifting into her kraken form as soon as she submerged. One by one, they climbed onto Urlanta's tentacles and were ferried to the other side of the river. The thick skin of her kraken form was rubbery and rather than feeling slick and slimy from the water, the surface felt almost sticky, allowing them to get across much easier than Suleima anticipated.

Once everyone was back on dry land, they returned to the cliff. An eerie fog crept over the low meadow, giving the creepy red castle an even more sinister appearance. "If this fog is a daily occurrence here, we may be able to use it for cover," Suleima observed.

After a bit of searching, she found a rough path, probably only used by animals, as it was extremely narrow. Suleima pulled her pack straps tighter and gripped the rocks of the cliff face as she led the way down the path.

The clip-clop of hooves caught her attention and she turned to see a blue-gray goat with glowing blue freckles on its cheeks, bouncing its way along the cliff face, quickly passing their group without hesitation. Urlanta's wings in this form were tucked tight against her body. Her goat form appeared smaller here than in the vision she showed when facing off against Solisa in the cavern. Nimbly loping from one impossibly narrow ledge to the next, Urlanta disappeared from sight quickly.

"Show off," muttered Dynasira. "If I could fly here, we'd have beat her to the bottom!"

Suleima giggled. "It's not a race, Dyna."

They carefully picked their way, with toes and fingertips the only things keeping them from plunging to the bottom. As they neared the waterfall, the surface became slippery. They made it to a ledge behind the waterfall, where Urlanta waited for them. They rested their weary fingers and feet on the widest ledge they'd come upon so far, while Urlanta danced around impatiently. They took a moment to refuel and inched their way off the ledge and out the other side of the waterfall.

A loud screech sounded over the din of the water, driving Urlanta back to them quickly. Touching her goat-like nose to Suleima's hand, Suleima saw a huge fae bird patrolling the cliff's edge.

Had someone seen them when they were on the cliff? Or was this a regular patrol? Or just a bird out for a flight?

Urlanta must have seen Suleima's thoughts as well, while they continued to touch, and she projected answers back to Suleima's mind. These were Solisa's birds. Whether on regular patrol or some other mission, Urlanta didn't know. But, if they were seen by the bird, they would lose any element of surprise.

"Will she know if we eliminate the bird?" Agron asked, after hearing the explanation from Suleima.

She waited a moment for Urlanta to show her the answer, then dropped her pack at her feet and gripped her bow. "It's not unusual for these birds to go far and wide. If it's not out here because someone saw us, then it could be gone for days before returning to the castle. If it's here because someone saw us, the element of surprise is already gone." Nocking an arrow, Suleima stepped to the edge of the waterfall, careful to keep her back glued to the wall behind her. "I believe she'll know if I use my magic, even here."

Suleima aimed carefully and loosed the arrow, grabbing and nocking a new one in the next breath. At the same instant the bird screeched, skittering away from the first arrow, Suleima loosed the second. She was nocking the third when a pained shriek sounded. The bird was hit in the wing near its shoulder and tumbled through the air, knocking against the cliff face as it fell.

Urlanta galloped out from the cover of the waterfall and bounded down the wall of rock. Another ear-piercing screech had Suleima hurrying to peer around the water and below. She stepped back quickly and suppressed a shudder, the image of the angry symbriole stomping on the injured bird with her sharp hooves burned into her brain. She gathered her pack and bow, motioning for the others to join her as she crept out onto the next extremely narrow edge on the side Urlanta had gone. Suleima did her best to keep her gaze focused on the handholds in front of her and the path she was headed, blocking out the image in her head left by the symbriole's vicious attack.

More fog had moved in as they approached the ledge she had seen when first peering down the cliff face and darkness was beginning to fall. They stopped on the ledge for a breather.

"I'm trying to decide which is more dangerous—taking the path in the dark and fog, effectively blind, or staying here until daybreak," Suleima said.

Urlanta appeared. She carried several loops of braided vines around her neck. She dropped them, touching her nose to Suleima's hand again. Suleima's vision shifted, showing them being led in a single file down the face, the symbriole leading the way.

As much as she was hesitant to continue, staying on the narrow ledge was too risky. Suleima tied the vines around each of her friends and herself before throwing a final coil around Urlanta's neck, "We aren't as spry and nimble on these rocks as you are. Please lead us slowly."

Not three steps out, Suleima lost her footing, and if not for Gage grabbing her by the waistband, she might have taken everyone down the steep cliff with her. Heart racing, Suleima gripped Gage tightly, her face buried in his shoulder as she sucked in great gulps of air to calm herself.

He was fine.

She was fine.

So was everyone else. She flexed her hands a few times, willing them to release Gage as her heart rate slowed.

"One step at a time. I won't let you fall," he whispered in her ear.

Her imperceptible nod was enough of an affirmative for him. He gave her one last squeeze and steadied her as she took her next tentative step.

It took much longer at their slower pace, but within a few hours, the last of their feet hit solid, flat ground. The thick pile of the grass cushioned their abused feet and the blisters on Suleima's hands and fingers had blisters of their own.

The fog licked at their feet, casting an eerie film over the entire meadow, but only reaching as high as their knees, not useful for any kind of cover. The waterfall fell into a pool, casting a spray of water high into the air. In the moonlight, the crystalline surface of the pool reflected off nearby rocks, the minerals within adding to the shine.

Now that they were at the bottom of the cliff face, the castle, still in the distance, towered above, impossibly high. The shiver running down Suleima's spine had nothing to do with the dampness in the air.

Chapter 25

Sunlight glinted off the spray of water from the waterfall, producing an array of cheerful rainbows, contrasting with their sour moods and the dangers they knew were ahead. Fog still lingered in the meadow, wispy and drifting through the grasses.

Suleima flexed her sore hands and feet. While she was healing faster than normal due to her bond with Gage, the tenderness remained. The trek through the grasses required much less physical strain, but with the lack of cover, her anxiety and emotional strain ratcheted into the stratosphere.

Gage would make the rest of the trip to the castle in his wolf form. He stayed at Suleima's hip as they hiked, bumping into her leg every time she tugged at her hair, pulling it in front of her scarred face.

The dragons did their best to make their human forms appear smaller, crouching as they walked. Urlanta stayed in her smaller goat form, her wings tucked tight against her body, hidden by the low-lying fog. Suleima kept her bow at the ready and her head on a swivel, taking in the sky, the meadow, and the castle in the distance. Fed from the pool under the waterfall, the river beside them babbled along. It stayed straight for as far as they could see it, but she knew from the view above the cliff that it would eventually turn and head straight to the castle. She wondered absently if it became some sort of moat, like out of a wild fairy tale.

If only they hadn't known what awaited them when they finally reached the castle, the softly rolling hills and valleys of the clearing surrounding the castle would have made for a peaceful walk. The castle appeared to sneer at them as they got closer.

No one spoke. Keeping their heads down, the group wandered ever closer to the castle. A thicker fog drifted in helping to hide them as they followed the curve of the river. The sky darkened and they picked up their pace. Under the cover of dark would be the safest time to approach the castle.

Hours later, Suleima wanted to laugh at the absurdity when she saw that the river did indeed become a moat.

A wood and stone bridge seemed the only way across the moat and into the castle.

A small outcropping of rock at the corner of the castle was large enough to keep them hidden, and they rested for a couple of hours.

As the first rays of the sun lightened the sky, Gage's low growl alerted her to a presence on the castle wall. Obscured by the dim light, Suleima couldn't tell what the creature was, only that he was armed with a sword and what looked like a slingshot. The sword clanged off his armor with each step he took, each rotation as he paced. The slingshot, or maybe a modified bow and arrow, was held at the ready as the soldier scanned the horizon. But he couldn't have been paying enough attention, because they had slipped in without him sounding off any alarm. Suleima looked away, not wanting her attention on the soldier to alert him to their presence.

Using the smallest bit of her magic, Suleima felt for any wards around the castle. It did nothing to assuage her worry when her scan showed nothing. Gage bumped her hip as Urlanta headed away from them, shifted into her kraken form, and silently scaled the wall the soldier stood on. For something so massive, there was absolute silence. A tentacle wrapped around the soldier's head, and a moment later, he was no longer in sight. Urlanta scrambled back down the other side and emerged from a door in front of the castle in her innocent-looking cherub form.

They raced into the courtyard. In stark contrast to the lush grass outside, the desert-like floor sparkled in the emerging light of the day. They moved about, sticking to the shadows and taking in the thick stone wall surrounding the courtyard and castle. The deep red and black decor of the castle chilled Suleima to the bone, and she unconsciously stepped closer to Gage.

They made their way along the perimeter of the courtyard, stopping just a few feet from the castle door. Suleima held up her hand to stop them from advancing further. In a voice only loud enough for the shifters to hear, Suleima said, "I'm going to reach out to see if I can find where others are in the castle. The use of my magic could bring them all down on our heads. Be prepared for anything."

After acknowledging they heard her, the entire group was on alert with Suleima at the front, bow in hand and ready to fire. With no cover to investigate further, they were going in the front doors before anyone could spot them. Suleima hurried up the stairs but stopped short as she reached for the handle. A pulse echoed against her left, less sensitive, hand. She reached into the outer pocket of her pack, where she'd been keeping the fae cloth. It felt cool to the touch and glided over her hand, but as she reached for the handle, Koa yanked at a handful of her hair.

His arms flailed wildly, gesturing back the way they had come, and his chittering screeched at a much higher pitch than normal.

Suleima stumbled down a step back toward the courtyard. Koa seemed happy about that move and taking another step in the direction confirmed it. She motioned for the others to follow as they backtracked. He tugged her to a stop about halfway back to the gate they had entered.

Looking around, Suleima saw nothing and whispered to Koa, trying to figure out what he wanted. She held out her hand with Koa perched on it and watched as he pushed with all his might against the wall. Agron shouldered his way between Suleima and the wall and shoved. A grinding noise sounded as the wall swung open, barely wide enough for Suleima to pass through. She motioned for the others to wait there a moment and climbed through the narrow opening. Just on the other side of the wall, the river/moat floated by.

When she returned to the courtyard, her armor of water was in place.

Gage eyed Koa warily.

Their bond buzzed with concern. When their eyes met, Suleima crouched and laid her hand on his scruff. Her voice barely a whisper, she said, "I think he has at least some of the memories of the Green Knight. I trust him."

Gage's gaze seemed skeptical, but he stepped back, allowing her to take the lead again.

The group crept back to the doors at the front of the castle. With the cloth covering her left hand and her bow in the other, Suleima turned the knob, doing her best to ignore the buzzing sensation, and pushed the door silently open.

The door opened into a pristine foyer with black and red checkered tiles lining the floors. Strange brocade wallpaper covered every surface of the walls and ceilings, the black background enhancing the blood-red pattern with gilded gold outlining. The matte black lighting fixtures had red shades and golden accents.

It was quiet inside.

Suleima felt Koa shiver against her neck but didn't dare take her eyes off her surroundings. A shimmer in her peripheral vision caught her attention, dragging her gaze to the left. The room to the left looked empty but for a few gaudy red and black chairs and sofas. The area rug in the center of the seating area was the same hideous color scheme as the rest of the castle they'd seen thus far, but it glinted where the light bounced off the gold. Something was off in the room. She pulled her bow up, drawing back the string, and in that moment, heard a tinkling giggle.

The lights winked out, leaving an unnatural darkness, like all the light in the world was sucked away. The tinkling giggle sounded again, this time from a different direction. Gage's body leaned into Suleima as a fierce growl erupted from him. There was no sense in continuing to try to hide.

Solisa knew they were there.

Suleima fired an arrow into the darkness at the nearest threat. A grunt sounded from that direction, but she was already firing another arrow at the opposite end of the entryway.

Her first target moved before she could react, ripping the bow from Suleima's hand. It was obviously injured, but not too severely.

Gage lashed out, snapping his jaws, the squeal of pain sounding right next to Suleima's ear.

She felt Dynasira reach out and grab the attacker, heard Agron clanging into things as he tried to get down the entryway to the second attacker.

She pushed past her reluctance and pulled an orb of air into her hand. Pushing with fire, the orb exploded into light, more powerful than she intended, but it drove both attackers a few steps back, as well as two new attackers they had missed in the darkness. Unfortunately, it also temporarily blinded herself and her allies.

As the spots cleared from her vision, Urlanta, now in her larger goat-like form joined Agron, stomping at the attacker, a red-skinned, fat sprite-like creature. Its wings were too small relative to its body size, to give it any ability to fy.

The third attacker, coming from the stairs, was nearly identical, but was rail thin and zipped this way and that, almost too fast to follow.

Dynasira's opponent had what was left of Suleima's arrow sticking from his shoulder and bright green blood dripping down the alabaster white skin on his leg from Gage's bite. The tinkling giggle, a stark contrast to his tall and muscular frame, still emerged from him as he fought Dynasira.

Everything about this creature was ghostly white. No color was visible in his eyes and with his lips peeled back in a snarl, even the inside of his mouth was pale white, only a small hint of green visible where Dynasira must have landed a blow, bloodying his lip.

The skinny sprite darted over, popping Suleima's light orb like a soap bubble with a finger, and they were once again plunged into darkness.

Suleima had a new orb ready and released it into the air as she swung her hand, swatting the sprite into the wall, successfully stunning her.

Between Agron and Urlanta, their attacker was down as well, but the fourth one, taller even than Dynasira's enemy and twice as muscular, released a great roar. His skin, red like the sprites, appeared to emit a glow as fire burned in his eyes. He focused on Suleima, batting Agron and Urlanta out of the way, their bodies slamming against the wall with an audible crack, sending plumes of dust into the air where Agron's shoulder penetrated the gaudy brocade wallpaper and into the structure of the wall beneath.

Gage snapped his jaws and dove down the entryway, aiming for the enormous creature. Gage slid through his legs, causing him to spin around, exposing his back and the tiniest set of wings. This behemoth was a sprite! An altered sprite, but a sprite just the same.

Suleima snatched her bow from the ground where it had landed and fired off two arrows in quick succession. They both bounced clean off the back of the enraged and altered sprite, smoldering by the time they hit the floor.

Gage nipped at him, keeping the sprite's attention on him.

Gliding a spare bit of water from her skin, Suleima worked air magic to form the water, as she'd done so many times before. This time, when her arrow fired, it sank in and hissed at the contact with the fire burning inside of the creature. She released the air magic holding its shape.

The mammoth sprite arched his back, howling in pain, and spun to face Suleima. The wide grimace on his mouth exposed sharply pointed and serrated teeth, yellowish-green in color. He gnashed them in her direction and took a menacing step toward her.

Gage locked the back of the sprite's calf in his jaw, only to be tossed into the wall. He landed hard against the wall with a small, pained yelp. Gage struggled to get back to his feet.

Suleima felt his pain. Rage skyrocketed within her, and she gathered more of her fae water, coaxing and molding it as she pulled on air to aid her. She splintered and shaped it, conjuring hundreds of needles of water. Pushing a gust of air behind them, she sent the needles hurtling through the space between them, slamming into the enraged sprite.

His wail of pain pierced the air. He stomped forward and batted Suleima like a bug, sending her into the next room where she slammed into the pretentious sofa, bruising the ribs where they connected with the ornate woodwork on the frame.

"Why the ribs?" she half coughed, half shouted. She struggled to stand upright.

Rib injuries were the worst.

The creature stalked into the room, coming ever closer, blood dripping from all of the tiny puncture wounds.

Suleima stood her ground.

Fighting against the urge to turn and run, Suleima planted her feet and waited.

When he was within reach, he grabbed her by her braid, twisting it into his hand and yanking her toward him. The moment her torso came in contact with his, he squealed.

Feeding fae magic into him, the water easily penetrated his wounds. He writhed in pain, yanking at her hair with each jerk of his body. Steam from the water now erupted from the pinpricks. Not wishing to prolong his suffering, Suleima called back the water in a swift move. The sprite collapsed at her feet.

Suleima sensed dozens of fae creatures surging onto the castle property from every direction. She ran back to the door and placed her hand on the frame, hastily constructing a ward. She mixed her fae and shamanistic magic in hopes of, at least, slowing down Solisa's army. Her knees were weak and dizziness overwhelmed her, but she shook it off and straightened, assessing the damage to her allies. She could feel Gage's pain, but he hid his limp.

A surge of power washed over her, nearly bringing her to her knees. Suleima braced herself against the wall as she scanned to see where the power was coming from.

The basement.

Chapter 26

SULEIMA STUMBLED DOWN THE hall and burst through the doors, landing in a grotesquely overdecorated dining room. All black, red, and gold, once again, the decor would be seizure-inducing on a good day. Already nauseated and dizzy from the waves of magic being sucked into the basement the busyness of the varying and contrasting patterns splattered around the room didn't help. She stumbled with a particularly strong wave but caught herself and shoved through the doors into a kitchen out of the same decorating handbook as the rest of the castle. The vast room had stone inset ovens and long stone troughs for grilling, where coals still gave off heat. Ornate filigree marred every surface imaginable. An absurd thought about how difficult it would be to clean with all those crevices and cracks crossed her mind.

The gold fixtures glinted, reflecting the light from her orb as it drifted ahead of them.

She grabbed at the stone island with the sink carved into it as more magic flowed and poured in from every direction. She spotted a heavy, reinforced metal and wood door at the far end of the kitchen and raced to it. She jerked at the door; it didn't budge, and the jolt she felt travel up her arm stole her breath.

Covering her hand in the fae cloth, Suleima reached again for the door. It still refused to budge.

Agron nudged her out of the way and directed her to stand back, giving her a stern look. "We need to get down there as soon as possible, right? This isn't the time for delicacy."

Dynasira herded them to the side, leaving enough room for Agron to shift.

He remained crouched, so as not to hit his head on the beams and ceiling. His massive jaw opened, and he dripped acid on the hinges at the side of the door. A moment later, his deep green hair and normal stature replaced the iridescent dragon scales and wings that took up a good portion of the room. He held his arm out, keeping Suleima from approaching while the acid ate away at the metal and magic holding the door closed.

When the last piece of hinge melted away, Agron's booted foot connected with the door and it blasted open, tumbling awkwardly down the stairs until it lodged between the ceiling and the stair treads. Agron tugged his foot back, shaking it and cursing.

Suleima pulled up a shield and raced down the stairs, careful to avoid touching the door, which still emanated magic despite the damage it had taken.

The stark stone walls and floor were a welcome contrast to the chaotic decor from the previous rooms. It should have been colder than the floor above, but it was sweltering. They entered another hallway, flanked on the sides by door after door. Cries and whimpers could be heard from behind some of them, but Suleima's gaze was locked on the blood-red door at the far end of the hall.

"Will you stay out here?" Suleima asked, already knowing their answer, but hoping to keep them as far out of harm's way as possible.

Gage's growl and Dynasira's raised eyebrow answered.

Urlanta stomped her hoof.

As they reached the end of the hallway, within just a few feet of the door, the ground beneath them shifted and buckled, knocking them off balance. Suleima slammed hard into one of the walls with her shoulder, jarring her already injured ribs, stealing her breath. Stars danced in her vision as she struggled to pull air into her lungs. Gage stumbled over to her with a low whine, pushing his muzzle into her hand, checking on her, and reassuring her. The ugly sconces shifted with the movement, some falling to the floor and shattering.

Using the cloth, Suleima lumbered forward awkwardly as the floor continued to pitch. The thick beams above groaned and cracked. "She's liable to bring the whole building down!" Suleima shouted, lunging the last few feet. She wrapped her hand around the knob, the angry buzzing under the fae cloth more intense than ever before.

A sudden chill against her back startled her. Suleima turned to face the stairs. Snowflakes swirled along the floor, as two delicately shod feet descended.

Soon, Zenisa stood at the foot of the stairs, unaffected by the swaying and shaking floor. Ice crystals formed at her feet as she walked toward them, freezing the earth below and slowing its movement. "Step aside." Icy wind snaked around their bodies and shoved them against the wall on either side of the hallway.

Ice shot forward, puncturing the wooden door. An instant later, it became rivulets of water, tracing the grain of the wood before pooling on the floor. Zenisa repeated her actions, with the same result.

Suleima used her earth magic to grip the floor and wrestled her way to stand in front of Zenisa.

Zenisa's wind battered her even harder, but she didn't budge, just adjusted her stance to withstand the onslaught. Gage snarled and snapped but couldn't get to her.

"Get out of my way!"

"If you can't get through the door with your magic alone, what makes you think you can take on your sister by yourself?" Suleima countered.

The intensity of Zenisa's icy stare rose. The wind increased, and the temperature dropped further.

"You can fight me first, but that weakens you against her."

Suleima waited calmly. Her shield was ready to be pulled at a moment's notice, but she hoped to not need it, yet.

The winds calmed enough for Suleima to release her hold on earth and for Gage and the others to step away from the walls.

They formed a guard around Suleima.

She stepped up to Gage's shoulder, resting her hand on his fur. She presented the illusion that she was calm and passive, not ready to throw her own spells if Zenisa pushed her too hard.

Zenisa eyed the group. Suleima wasn't sure if she was trying to figure out a way to work with them, or a way to go *through* them.

"We can stand here all day, but while we do, your sister is going to try her best to destroy the world as we know it. Ready to work together?"

Zenisa hesitated and Suleima flexed her hand. Noticing the movement, Zenisa nodded uneasily.

Suleima turned to face the door, but the others kept Zenisa in their sights.

"We've run into very few wards, other than the magic on the doors. Any idea why?" Dynasira asked.

"Solisa rules by fear. Her fae would be too afraid to enter without her explicit invitation. She's also arrogant."

Agron cleared his throat, earning him a scathing look.

Zenisa continued. "In addition, while our magic is virtually limitless, using a lot at once does tire us. If she's going to use the spells in that book, she's going to need a lot of power. It will weaken her."

Suleima stepped closer to the door. With the fae cloth wrapped around her hand, she reached for the handle.

Since the hinges were on the other side of the door, Agron's fancy trick with his acid wouldn't work this time.

She prodded the magic in the door with her own. Sending pulses of both her shamanistic magic and her fae magic, she searched for differences anywhere.

Dead center of the door at her eye level is where she found it. Of course it was. The symbol Dirrin had burned into his bedroom door at Erist's home, the one that protected his room from the inferno he'd set the day he killed Erist. It was hidden not *on* the door, but within the wood. It pulsed back at her when her shamanistic magic drifted over it. "Stand to the sides, please," she said, turning to Gage. "I think I can open it with fire."

A great clatter on the stairs behind them alerted them that they were no longer alone in the hallway.

"Open it!" Zenisa demanded as she spun to face the stairs, balls of ice forming in her palms.

More of the altered sprites rushed forward, all of them different from each other, as if Solisa hadn't found the best way to alter them yet.

The commotion of the fight behind her was a distraction she couldn't afford, so she blocked it out and refocused on the door. She flexed her fingers and cleared her mind. A flame on the other side called to her and she reached for it. She pulled it straight to herself. When the magic of the flame hit the door, it hissed and sizzled, but continued through.

Sweat beaded on her brow. Directing fire required a finesse she hadn't practiced in years.

The spark of fire inside the door now, Suleima sensed the heat and pulse of the ember. Pushing and pulling, she guided the ember within the confines of the wood, tracing along the grain until it reached the bottom edge of the symbol.

Suleima pulled a shield in front of her and yelled, "Duck!"

Calling with not only the fire magic she held within her, but also with the connection to Volos through Gage, Suleima jerked at the flame.

The door exploded, sending wood and metal shrapnel flying at them. Despite the shield in front of them, Suleima flinched and turned away, yanking up another shield to cover her allies, but not high enough to protect the altered sprites.

They were impaled.

Smoke and dust filled the doorway. An eerie red and purple glow permeated the debris floating in the air. A shadowed figure soon became clear.

Chapter 27

Behind her, Suleima heard Gage, Dynasira, and Agron reengaged with the sprites still fighting, but the icy chill at her back told her Zenisa had shifted her focus to her sister's shadow. Urlanta, standing next to her now, stomped a hoof and lowered her head, the horns on her head shifting and growing, abnormally large now, and the points sharpening.

With barely a twitch, Urlanta was gone, charging into the room still clearing of debris. The impact of Urlanta's horns on the bubble-like shield surrounding Solisa sent reverberations through the air and stunned the symbiole, who stumbled to the side, shaking her head.

"You're too late!" Solisa cackled. "I've set the spell in motion. It is only a matter of time."

As if to affirm her statement, the ground pitched and waved anew, the stone foundation groaning with each roll and sway. A collection of boulders from the back wall of the castle tumbled to the floor, opening a window into the meadow beyond. They watched as a great fissure opened, spewing sand and dirt into the air, creating a staggering-sized geyser.

Solisa zeroed in on Suleima, "Why aren't you back with your jinn? I know you found him. You left him, encased in stone for all eternity! I never thought you'd leave a friend in peril." Solisa's sneer taunted her.

"He's safe. And once I stop you, I won't stop until Hamanad is free."

Solisa grinned, though the strain of the spell made it more of a grimace. "You should have stayed with your friend. At least then, you would survive a few more weeks, instead of dying today." Solisa's hand waved as she cast, drawing attention to the severe burns covering the skin there. The damage to her hand was significant, but it didn't slow her down. She continued pulling and shaping the power of the spell.

Enraged she couldn't get to Solisa, Urlanta jumped from spot to spot, upending tables of ingredients, spell books, and beakers of unknown liquids, some melting through whatever they touched, others bubbling on the surfaces, and still others lying in a harmless puddle.

At one such landing, near where Suleima stood, Urlanta triggered some sort of trap.

Solisa laughed.

Suleima felt the swell of the power beginning. Launching herself in front of Urlanta, Suleima took a shot of what looked like lava straight to her chest. Steam rose from the shield covering her chest, enveloped her face, and heat seeped through the shield.

Solisa turned her attention to Zenisa.

Pulling from her fae water, Suleima replenished the shield's weakened spots after the lava damage.

Suleima nearly doubled over a moment later. Pain rippled across her hip. She turned to see Gage in the air, held by another colossal sprite. Dynasira rushed in to help him, hitting the sprite full force with her shoulder and slowing Gage's fall to the floor. He immediately re-engaged, only a slight limp marring his otherwise graceful movements.

Suleima turned back to the threat in front of her, focusing on her own fight.

"Oh, dear sister," Solisa taunted. "You came to watch me do what you will never be strong enough to do—rule over all. How sweet!"

The temperature in the room dropped drastically and Solisa's eyes blazed in response.

"Oh, sister dear," Zenisa said, sneering at Solisa, "Can't do much to us with the amount of power you're using." She raised a mocking eyebrow. "Tsk, tsk."

Suleima shivered. The temperature fell, the spilled liquids turning to ice on the stone floor, making the surface slick. Suleima pulled with earth, giving herself traction on the floor as she moved away from Zenisa, whose icy eyes were a paler blue than usual, almost completely white. Aggressive wind blew only for Zenisa whipping her hair around her head in a cloudburst of chaos.

Zenisa laughed, but Solisa didn't slow. She turned a page in the book and chanted nonsensical words, nearly too low for Suleima to hear over the cacophony of the noises. The sun outside blazed hotter, having risen high into the sky while they were fighting inside. The push and pull of the temperatures warred against one another where the stones had fallen. The sand geyser stopped for a moment but erupted anew. This time, reddish-orange lava spouted high into the air, dropping onto the mound of sand left behind and rolling in all directions. Steam rose as the grasses of the meadow burned away.

While Solisa and Zenisa were focused on each other, Suleima crept slowly toward the other side of the room, where Urlanta had stopped smashing things, and watched the stand-off impatiently, stomping her hooves in frustration. Suleima kept her eyes peeled for any hint of a weakness in the bubble surrounding Solisa. She quietly poked with her magic, as she made her way around the room.

The book was inside the bubble, and she needed to get it. The key though, it lay on the one table Urlanta hadn't been able to upend. Even with all the other magic swirling through the room, the key stood out, its own magic pulsing.

"I'll make my way through this kingdom and the next, picking my way through, destroying everything and everyone in my path who will not bow down to me. I'd intended to save you for last, dear sister, so you could watch in horror, knowing there is nothing you can do to stop me. But, since you've practically presented yourself with a bow, I'll save you the agony of anticipation and take you out now. Here, in *my* kingdom."

"How disappointed Mother and Father would be to see it come to this. This *territory* was their pride and joy. Our opposites make us stronger and are not our enemy. There is no place for kingdoms. Certainly not *your* kind of kingdom."

Realizing Suleima was now behind her, Solisa spun, hatred filling her eyes. She looked Suleima up and down, sneering. "Ah, the scars Dirrin left. You're not hiding them? You dare to show your weakness, *your ugliness*, to the world?"

She fought down the urge to pull up her glamor. Holding on to all the times Gage told her she didn't need the glamor, Suleima steeled her spine. "My ugliness, as you call it, is only skin deep. I can't say the same for you." Punctuating her sentence, Suleima uprooted the stone beneath Solisa's feet, knocking her off balance and into the bubble around her, the bubble which only encased her to the floor, the bottom left open for Suleima to exploit.

Zenisa laughed. "An insignificant shaman has knocked you around. How shameful."

Solisa regained her feet, fire blazing in her eyes as she chanted from the book.

The floor beneath Suleima's feet buckled with enough force to throw her clear to the other side of the room, her left shoulder slamming against the leg of an upturned table. Numbness radiated down her arm and a stream of blood cascaded down her back, pooling at the waistband of her jeans, unhampered by the fabric of her shirt, now torn as badly as her skin.

Koa was thrown away from her, landing in the doorway to the hall. The jolt knocked the wind out of her, leaving her unable to shout a warning to Koa as an altered sprite put him in its sights and attacked. A split second later, Gage stood in the path of the sprite, blocking it from getting to Koa. Gage's teeth gnashed, his growls vicious, as he drove the sprite away.

Urlanta jumped over the lava beginning to drip into the room from the opening, her hooves slipping and sliding before she managed to get them under her. The lava popped and sizzled as it encountered the ice formed on the stone floor, blackening before more of the orange sludge poured over, repeating the process. Suleima and Urlanta skittered backward, slipping and sliding the entire way, fighting to retreat from the encroaching goo.

A blast of ice shattered against the lava, crusting the top with black as it supercooled, but within seconds bright orange cracks formed, fighting to invade the room further.

The temperature rose. Sweat poured off Zenisa, the heat of the lava successfully countering her cooling magic.

Suleima covered the wound with her right hand, attempting to staunch the flow of blood from her shoulder as her vision got sparkly. She heard the continued fighting of Gage and the others out in the hallway, sensing the altered sprites and others pouring down the stairs one after the other.

His worry for her bled through their bond.

Suleima flexed her fingers and ignored her fears. Pulling from deep within, she reached for her fire as Solisa's eyes blazed hotter. Her fear of the power of fire tightened her chest with anxiety. She struggled to pull in a full breath but redoubled her effort as Gage's pain radiated across their bond. He took yet another vicious blow.

Suleima gripped onto the fire she held within, leaning forward as she scanned Solisa. Deep within Solisa's gut, she found the root of her fae fire and that's where she aimed. Shoving as hard as she could, Suleima pushed her fire through the floor, the weakness in Solisa's bubble, and pumped her magic in, like when Erist had taught her to boil water within a closed can from the inside out. Solisa was her can.

Worry crossed Solisa's face, then determination. Solisa gathered the increase of magic to her, and a wave of dizziness washed over Suleima. The pressure in the bubble increased and Suleima threw herself in front of Urlanta a split second before the bubble burst and the world went black.

Chapter 28

A ROUGH, WET TONGUE slid over her face. "Ugh! Enough!" She moved to wipe the wolf drool from her face.

Then came the blinding pain.

Her entire body was on fire. Her head throbbed. Sticky blood still dripped, more slowly than before, down her back, and her stomach threatened to revolt. She could no longer physically feel the floor rippling and tossing, but in her head, some roller coaster zoomed around with her locked inside while the room spun.

Opening her eyes just a slit, sunlight blinded her and made her head throb more intensely. A pile of rubble delineated the room where Solisa had been casting from the large hallway where Gage, Dynasira, and Agron had fought. The doors lining the hallway were demolished. Nothing more remained than splinters littering the floors and small chunks hanging listlessly from the metal hinges. The few rooms she could see into from her vantage point were empty but for a threadbare, thin, hay-stuffed, filthy mattress on the floor. Blood and who knows what else covered the floors and walls.

Gage's fur was matted and caked with blood. Dynasira's clothes were ripped and there were rapidly healing cuts on her face and arms. Agron's eye must have been cut but had already healed to a sickly greenish-yellow. The symbriole sat on the floor, in her innocent-looking cherub form, almost pouting, with no visible injuries in sight. Zenisa seemed no worse for the wear, but a dullness echoed in her eyes as she stared at the last place Suleima had seen Solisa.

Suleima tried to move to stand, but her body protested, forcing her to remain where she was. "What happened?"

"Whatever you did, it overloaded the spell Solisa was casting. Her power ricocheted inside the bubble, too much for either her or the spell, or both." Zenisa's voice was hollow.

"I'm sorry." Those insufficient words were the only ones that came to her mind as she looked at Zenisa.

"The book, what's left of it at least, is there," Zenisa pointed to a charred clump on the far side of the room. "Someone needs to check on the fae in this territory. With Solisa gone, there will be chaos. And someone needs to check on the damage in the area, see how far-reaching it is." There was zero inflection in her voice.

Suleima tried to stand again. She made it to her feet, but the process wasn't pretty. "Let us help you..."

The emphasis in her voice this time was plain, as she commanded, "No!" She cleared her throat; her eyes latched onto Suleima. "You will leave this place as soon as possible. Take the book with you. Get it and yourselves out of my sight." The temperature in the room dropped significantly. "I have lost enough since you came into my life." The ice in her eyes shimmered for a moment. "With Solisa gone, the protections over this place will have fallen with her. You can fly out of here. You can land to rest, but get out of this territory without hesitation."

Zenisa spun, her icy blue skirt twirling around her, and left by way of the now precarious-looking set of stairs at the far end of the hallway.

Gage shifted, mottled bruises visible on his ribs, hip, and shoulder. He quickly dressed in clothes Suleima kept in her pack for him. "Let me look at your shoulder."

"Later." Suleima, with a limp in her gait, walked over to where the charred remains of the book lay. She flipped the pages of the still open book, inspecting it. The exterior was demolished, flaking off in hunks of charred remnants. Most of the spells remained intact, but one, presumably the one Solisa used was blackened and unreadable. She closed the book, inspecting the exterior, and felt a mechanical click. The book was once again locked closed. Using the fae cloth, Suleima picked up the key, which still pulsed with its own magic, carefully wrapping it and the book together and adding it to the contents of her pack.

"Zenisa just said Solisa's protection spells around her territory died with her. Does that mean...?" Dynasira asked.

"That Hamanad has been freed?" Suleima replied. "I hope so." She ignored the pain in her shoulder and ribs as she pulled the pack onto her back and turned.

"Ready?" Gage asked.

Suleima nodded. The exhausted group hobbled their way through the ruins of the basement hallway and stepped carefully up the stairs. As they entered the kitchen area, the destruction was staggering. Sunlight streamed in from holes in the walls, ceilings, and floors above. The wide window looking out over the meadow revealed tall piles of sand from the geysers that appeared, scorched earth and grass, and lava flows still glowing hot through the cracked black surface. Beyond the castle, trees on this side of the meadow tipped and tilted, sheared off in places, some with all their needles and leaves torn away.

Solisa had not only destroyed the castle and the land surrounding it. Suleima shook her head. Madness. Had her plan been successful, Solisa would have ruled over ruins.

They walked back the way they entered; frames lay scattered on the floor. Their steps crunched over shards of broken glass. The dark wood floors were buckled and warped. The hideous furniture was tossed and tipped. Cushions peppered the floor in the sitting room. The massive door they'd entered hung drunkenly off the one hinge remaining. The concrete railing and stairs leading up to the door were crumbling. The stairs no longer matched up; a fissure had opened down the center, and one side of the steps lifted over a foot higher than the other side.

Urlanta stepped up beside Suleima and grabbed her hand, the vision overwhelming the destruction in front of her.

The symbriole's anger and frustration bloomed in Suleima's chest, at her inability to reach Solisa, then the disappointment that she didn't get to take her own shot at the mad fae. The destruction in front of her slowly transformed, remaking the castle ruins, the meadow, and the lands beyond into the paradise it once was—the paradise it was always meant to be. Fae came together, no longer afraid, willing to work with one another—Urlanta, reuniting with her people, fae of all kinds, gathering, combining forces, and remaking the fae lands to suit all of their needs

When the vision receded, Suleima wiped a tear from her cheek and watched Urlanta shift into her goat-like form and trot off across the courtyard, leaping the impossible distance over the moat and into the meadow beyond. Her wings spread wide as she glided over it gracefully. She waved at the symbriole's retreating form and turned to her friends. "She's going to the fae who live in these lands, to help them rebuild. It's safe for her here now."

Suleima welcomed Gage's steadying hand on her arm as she picked her way down the stairs and into the courtyard. The walls around the perimeter were missing giant chunks of rock, and the bridge they crossed to get over the moat lay in pieces.

Before she could turn to Dynasira, the blue dragon shifted and stretched, the scales along her spine clicking as she stretched. Agron followed suit. Lifting off, Dynasira grabbed Suleima, and Agron picked up Gage.

As they sailed above the meadow, the scope of the damage was revealed.

Sections of the riverbed had shifted several feet, disturbing the natural flow and causing rapids in places and flooding in others. The cliff-face they had climbed down...whole sections of it had sheared off and crashed to the earth below, leaving piles of rubble and debris and great craters in their wake.

Lava erupted far from Solisa's castle and started massive wildfires. Flames licked at the trees at the top of the cliff. Dynasira dipped lower, dousing the flames with her water, then banked off to the side to hit another area affected. They could see fae moving below, coming out of their hidden houses and assessing the damage. It would take so much work to rebuild.

The distance the spell traveled was astonishing. They were well beyond two day's walk from the castle when the terrain finally looked undisturbed.

Suleima's tears fell.

Chapter 29

Darkness surrounded them when Dynasira and Agron landed. Despite their exhaustion and weariness, they set up camp for the night. Suleima set up her tent and ushered the dragons into it after feeding them. "You need the rest more than us right now," Suleima said when Dynasira began to protest. "You're flying us home. No arguments. Go."

Once they were tucked away inside the tent, Suleima put up a ward and sat next to Gage at the fire. Koa remained at Gage's side, leaning against his boot as he dozed.

He wrapped his arm around her shoulder, pulling her closer, and breathed in her scent. "How are you?"

"Like everyone, I'm tired. But otherwise, I'm fine."

"Liar," he teased, tightening his hold on her.

"I feel bad, like I always do. Each loss of life—it haunts me." She paused a moment. "I still don't understand. I know what I did, magically speaking, but I don't know how or why it worked."

"Can you explain it to me? Maybe that will help you figure it out."

"Erist used to make me try to boil water in a sealed can. The pressure builds up and expands. A body can only handle so much magic at once. Solisa was using so much power to fuel the spell. I thought if I pushed her more, forced her to filter through more magic, she would have to stop the spell to correct the flow. But, instead of stopping she tried to use my magic to... I don't know. I thought if I introduced shamanistic magic, it would interrupt the flow of her fae magic. I pushed my magic into her, just like I would have the can."

"You have a unique ability to blend shamanistic magic with fae magic," Zenisa said, emerging from the woods, but stopping at the barrier ward Suleima placed.

Gage's hold on her tightened and a low growl rumbled in his chest as he stared at the Ice Goddess. Suleima placed her hand on his thigh. His muscles coiled and bunched under her grasp.

Koa stirred a bit, attracting Zenisa's eye, but Suleima sat forward, blocking the young fae from Zenisa's line of sight.

Zenisa smirked, then eyed Gage, cracking her wrists, like she herself was preparing to fight. "I believe Solisa thought she was powerful enough to take your magic and use it. She was obviously wrong." Zenisa's eyes drifted to the tent. Her voice was cold. "Be in the air by first light. You shouldn't need to land in this area again. Be clear of it before nightfall tomorrow." A blink of an eye later, Zenisa was gone.

"Is she going to be a problem?" Gage asked, his voice quiet.

Zenisa's laughter echoed in the distance.

"I hope not." Suleima squeezed his hand. She laid her other hand on the flap of her pack. Even through the heavy canvas of the pack and the fae cloth, the magic of the key buzzed eagerly at her touch.

Suleima fought off the guilt at dozing occasionally, since Gage spent the night as a wolf. She rolled to her feet, making sure she didn't disturb Koa, who was curled up next to Gage's muzzle. Gage's ears twitched as he listened for approaching danger. She patted Gage's head, prepared a quick breakfast, and woke the dragons to tell them about their visit from the Ice Goddess and her directive that they get going and be out of the area by nightfall.

The group flew high above the trees, not stopping until they crossed the border of the fae lands. The dragons dropped heavily to the ground and shifted. Dark circles marred the skin around their eyes. Their shoulders drooped and footsteps landed hard as they trudged to the center of the clearing.

Suleima set about preparing camp again, getting a fire started and giving them some food rations to tide the dragons over until Gage returned from the hunt he'd started as soon as they'd landed. Koa danced around, making Dynasira and Agron giggle at his antics while Suleima set up the tent again.

When Suleima sat to clean and cook Gage's catch, Dynasira asked, "Why is Zenisa so upset? Did she not realize this was the likely outcome?"

"It's one thing to guess at an outcome, to know that your actions will contribute to a likely death. It's another thing entirely to witness the death of someone you were once close to, even someone who has done horrible things." Gage's hand stalled her movements as she spoke, taking the knife from her to finish. "It seems like we've been fighting this same battle for years. Dirrin—while it seems so long ago on one hand, on the other, his death is as close as yesterday. Dirrin needed to die. Kylin needed to die. Solisa's death was inevitable. She influenced them both. Being directly responsible for the deaths of two of my childhood friends, one who was like a brother to me..." Suleima stared hard at her blood-covered hands, realizing how it mirrored the horror she felt. "I'll never wash myself clean of the guilt. Dirrin was only 'like a brother.' Not only was Solisa truly Zenisa's sister, but she was also her twin. The hardship Zenisa is facing—I don't envy it."

"As always, you are more forgiving than I would be," Dynasira responded.

"And yet Yanima still lives." Suleima raised her eyebrows at her friend, who had the sense to look a bit sheepish.

"Touché." Dynasira was quiet for a moment before she spoke again, her words barely above a whisper. "It's not as easy to take a life outside of battle. In the heat of the moment, you are fighting for your life. You do what you must do to survive, to save those you care about. After..."

Suleima nodded.

The four of them stared quietly into the flames as they watched the meat from Gage's hunt cook. Even Koa stopped his crazy antics and sat quietly, sensing the needs of the group.

In a repeat of the previous night, Suleima shooed the dragons to sleep in the tent after filling their bellies and she and Gage took over the night's watch. Tomorrow, they would reach Pila's encampment before nightfall.

A small smile stole over Suleima's face.

"What are you thinking about over here?" Gage asked, pulling her against him as he sat down.

"Reuniting with our friends, the pack, and seeing Hamanad again." She closed her eyes, leaning into the warmth and comfort he offered.

Chapter 30

With a straight shot to the jinn tribe lands and Dynasira and Agron flying at top speed, they landed to an audience of their friends by mid-afternoon.

They were swarmed with greetings the moment their feet hit the ground. Pila and Jonah remained off to the side, while the others converged on them the second the dragons shifted to their smaller, human size.

Suleima's eyes darted over the gathered friends—there was a distinct absence. "Where's Hamanad?" she asked.

Faramad and Tiamaned fidgeted with impatience.

"He'd still locked in stone," Nadiram replied, confusion marring her expression. "Where else would he be?"

Suleima's stomach dropped; they'd been wrong. "Solisa's protections over the fae lands she ruled dissolved once she died. We hoped it would be the same with Hamanad."

She lifted the remains of the book and the key from her pack. "I've not had time, or light to examine the book until now, but I promise to work until I have an answer. We *will* release Hamanad." She turned to Pila. "Once Hamanad has been freed, a decision needs to be made on how to protect this book and the key again."

Pila dipped her head in a single nod. She stepped away from Jonah and led the way into the hut where Hamanad remained.

The hut was dark inside, but Pila lifted the canvas window coverings, letting in the natural light. She lit several golden sconces around the main room.

Suleima sat heavily on a chair at the table in the kitchen area; Hamanad took up much of the large table in the dining area where he still lay, encased in stone. She delicately unwrapped the charred book, careful not to touch the key which buzzed incessantly.

Pila stepped up to the table and lay her hand over the key. Magic pulsed in the air, and suddenly the key lay quietly. She picked the key up and laid it in Suleima's hand.

It felt cool to the touch, no hint of the buzzing remained. The tarnished brass, worn smooth with age, appeared innocuous now, looking like any old skeleton key for any random antique door.

Suleima gently lifted the book, turning it this way and that, wondering how the key worked to unlock it. When she turned the book upright, with the spine facing her, a glint caught her eye. Upon closer examination, Suleima could barely make out the shape of the key outlined there. She turned the key, so it matched up with the spine and pressed it into place. The answering mechanical click she'd heard in the basement when she closed the book, sounded again. The vibration buzzed through her arm. But the book still remained locked. Suleima raised her eyes to Pila who stepped forward again.

She removed the key and set it to the side. Only then did the book open freely. That must be why the key wasn't in the book when they found Solisa in the basement.

Pila gasped at the sight of the charred pages within.

"I think the pages that are so badly damaged are the ones Solisa was using. The other pages are only charred on the edges," Gage explained.

Suleima gently turned page after page, scanning the contents for the spell they were all searching for so hopefully.

Dynasira spoke up from the doorway. "If the spell on Hamanad is fae, and the spells in the book fae, how did it come to be in the possession of the jinn?"

When Suleima looked up, Pila spoke. "All magic is rooted in the elements. The differences are in the way we access our magic; the way you access yours. But when boiled down to pure simplicity, it is all connected." She sat next to Suleima at the table and flipped to the destroyed pages of the book, trailing her fingers over it. "The stories tell us that when the spell was first used, it was the jinn who stood against the wielder. But only some of them. It is what split our tribes. The book and key were separated to keep them from being used again. While the spell inside, the one the fae were after, is incredibly dangerous, there are other spells contained within which are useful. I don't truly understand why the useful spells weren't taken out and the awful ones destroyed, but this was centuries ago. Any jinn with direct knowledge of the book and key are long dead."

"The spell Solisa used—it is charred beyond any readability, but it's not gone, is it?"

Pila shook her head. "There are ways to bring it back."

"And the spell we need to free Hamanad?"

"It is a disruption spell. More powerful than any of the jinn I have encountered could perform without the aid of the book. You should be able to perform the spell, Suleima. But it will take a lot of magic."

Dynasira lifted a hand. When Suleima nodded, she spoke. "The spells protecting the fae lands, the ones keeping Agron and I from landing there, fell when Solisa died. How is it that Hamanad is still trapped? I mean, Solisa set the spell. Shouldn't it have fallen with her?"

"The spell used to trap Hamanad is much more complicated than those protection spells would be my guess," Pila answered. "While I don't know the true reason for sure, it would be my best guess."

Suleima refocused on the spell book and flipped the pages.

The writing shifted like in the book Zenisa had shown her when they were figuring out how to rework Kylin's spell against her. As she flipped the pages, the scrambled letters and symbols shifted and adjusted until they became readable.

"The book shows itself to whoever possesses the key," Pila commented, answering Suleima's unasked question.

She flipped past a spell, then turned back to it, taking a moment to reexamine it. Cleansing The word pulsed in and out of focus, like the others, but it stuck out to her—called to her. She skimmed the spell, taking her time and making sure she truly understood the spell and each of the intentions behind it.

Suleima picked up her pack and pulled out the supplies she used to replenish her magic, placing them on the table. Running her hand over each vial reverently, she let her eyes drift over to where Gage stood. "This is going to require most of the reserves I have left. He won't awaken immediately," she explained. "It will likely be a few hours." She turned to Faramad and Tiamaned. "He will need healing when he comes out of it. His body has been slowed, but even so, without food and water for this length of time, he will be weakened."

Dynasira placed her hand on Suleima's shoulder. "Work the spell and then recharge. We can take it from there."

The world fell away as Suleima worked the complicated spell, her elements coming easily to her call despite the limited amount left in her reserves. She hadn't wanted to leave Gage alone as the sole protection while the dragons rested on their journey home, so she had put off recharging. Weariness dragged at her, but she fought through. Suleima siphoned her magic, as Erist had shown her, while she worked to free someone who filled in as her father figure, since Erist's passing. Hamanad had been there, quietly supporting her, giving her strength, and using his uncanny ability to suss out information to help her in any way he could.

A single tear ran down her cheek as she closed the spell and the book, feeling it lock again. Pila took the key and Jonah took the book, separating them, while Gage helped Suleima to her feet. Dynasira gathered the pack and Suleima's ingredients, following Gage into the next room, where she set the ingredients on a small table before returning to keep vigil at Hamanad's side.

The weight of her exhaustion dragged at her, but Suleima sluggishly completed her recharging ritual. As the last sparkles fell around her, Suleima's eyes drooped heavily, and Gage lifted her into his arms and lay beside her, drifting off before her head hit the pillow.

Chapter 31

Sounds of laughter registered in the darkness. As she tried to move, a heavy weight held her in place, muscles all over her body twinging in protest at the attempt. Gage's low growl in her ear made her smile.

"Rest. All is well. Rest now."

A smile played across her lips as she twisted her body to face her mate. "It worked?" she asked hopefully.

"You won't sleep more until you know, huh?" he answered, his gruff and sleepy laugh sending a thrill along her skin.

"He's ok?" she prompted, her eyes pleading.

"Fine." He laughed. "Go see for yourself." Gage raised his arm, giving her the freedom to move.

She stifled a groan as each bump, bruise, cut, and overworked, strained muscle protested at the speed with which she moved.

Moving much faster than she could, Gage came around to her side of the bed and helped her the rest of the way up. He kept his arm around her, steadying her as she walked to the doorway, finding the joyous sight in front of her.

Hamanad, looking much skinnier than before, wore a broad smile as he talked with Tiamaned, his arm slung around Faramad as they laughed and joked. The stress removed from Faramad's face, he looked years younger as he stood with his dad, the smile on his face filled with pure elation. They laughed with Dynasira and Agron.

Gage left her side to check on Kaly and Ryan who were embroiled in a card game, while Koa danced around on their table, kicking at the cards every chance he got.

Suleima walked forward a pace, catching Hamanad's attention. His grin split his face and he came over and bowed to her. He straightened, stepped forward, and hugged her to him. "I knew you could figure it out. If anyone could, it would be you." He dipped his head again and stepped back a pace.

"On my own, you would probably still be a statue," she replied shyly. "How are you feeling?"

He stretched a bit, his clothes hanging on his body, too large for him now. "I wasn't aware while trapped in that spell, thankfully. I think I'd have gone mad knowing the danger you and the others would be walking into without being able to help."

She lifted her gaze to take in the happiness around her, then continued their conversation. "Faramad, Tiamaned, and Nadiram were instrumental in helping us. Their skills in healing and disruption came in handy more than once." She winked at Faramad, pointing in his direction. "He's not the small child you portray him as."

Hamanad looked sheepish. "I'm proud of my boy. But he'll always be just a boy to me." He lifted his hand, tilting her face back and forth. "It looks like you had a tough battle. I'm sorry I wasn't there to aid you." Sadness coated his voice.

"The threat of Solisa is gone. Zenisa said she would help the fae in Solisa's territory. A symbriole from the caverns helped us. She also stayed behind with the other fae to help them rebuild."

"Can we anticipate the fae joining us on the Council of Erist?"

She shrugged. "I honestly doubt it." She paused in thought. "I would venture to assume the fae will continue to want to live in isolation. The option will always be open to them if they choose to take it."

Hamanad closed his hands around Suleima's. "Erist was proud of you before, but seeing you now, your growth, and your inclusion of others—he's smiling at you from the beyond."

Tears clouded her eyes as Hamanad spoke. He gave her another quick hug, then returned to the dragons and jinn. Her eyes followed him as he walked across the room, keenly aware of the frailty left behind after his entrapment.

Dynasira approached her, placing a hand on her shoulder. "Hamanad is going to be fine." She tipped her head in his direction. "Faramad is making sure he doesn't overdo anything. I think Hamanad is getting a taste of how he has hovered over Faramad over the years."

They laughed together as Faramad helped his father into a chair and scolded him for being on his feet so long while talking to Suleima, while Hamanad huffed at the babying treatment.

A softness in her voice, Dynasira spoke when their laughter died down, "You did good, Sul."

Suleima looked closely at her friend. The swirling mix of relief, sadness, and elation she saw in Dynasira's eyes mirrored her own feelings. "It's hard to be the ones left at the end of the battle. To celebrate the win but also mourn the loss of so many. The senseless deaths these last years of allies and foes alike—it was so unnecessary."

Dynasira shifted to face her directly. "We did what we had to do to save as many lives as possible." She grew quiet, her eyes sweeping the room. "I'd do it all again if it meant getting here." Her gaze turned sharply back to Suleima. "As long as I could do it with you."

Suleima hugged her friend tightly, Dynasira's royal blue hair tickling her nose. "Must you all bring tears to my eyes?" She cleared her throat. "I couldn't have done any of this without you. I'd have never made it beyond the first battlefield."

"Oh, so now it's your turn to make me cry?" Another hug and laughter had Dynasira slipping away to rejoin Agron and the jinn.

When she turned her head, Jonah stood there.

"He seems like a good Alpha. Not like Henry," he observed quietly.

"He *is* a good Alpha. A good man," she confirmed. "He would welcome you into his pack, Jonah."

Jonah shook his head. "I might like to come visit sometime. But a pack, no. I'm happy as a lone wolf."

"I would love it if you came to visit." Suleima squeezed his forearm. "Whenever you are ready."

Jonah's eye drifted to Pila. "She's said I can stay here within their territory. They don't have many warriors anymore. As isolated as they have been, there hasn't been a need."

"You will be a great asset to the tribe, Jonah. You taught me, and I will forever be grateful."

Jonah crept back into the shadows and Gage rejoined her.

"This peaceful feeling—let's hang onto it for a while," Gage said, wrapping his arms around her from behind.

"That is an order I would be oh so happy to follow."

The End

Thank you for joining me on this amazing adventure through the Amber Mountains and beyond! If you enjoyed the series, please leave me a review. Reviews are social proof to potential new readers and can be the difference between them taking a chance on a new book and not.

"What's next?" you ask. All the things! Lots of new and shiny ideas are bouncing around in my head. I have many more adventures to go on and imaginary friends to meet. Head over to jillianbeane.com and sign up for my newsletter to get updates on upcoming projects.

"Will we ever revisit the Amber Mountain crew again?" It's possible. A few secondary characters are clamoring for their moment in the spotlight. But for now, I think we are headed to a small town with a ranch, cowboys, horses and a sprinkle of suspense. After that, what happens when you splice the DNA of a woman with a Komodo dragon? How about a man with a shark or a panther? I'm having a fantastic time on these new adventures and I hope you'll come join me there too!

Acknowledgements

First, thank you to all of you who have read this book through to the end. Thank you for coming along on this journey with me! I truly hope you enjoyed it. Hopefully there will be many more adventures together in our futures!

This series would have never been possible without the support of my amazing husband and beautiful daughters. I can never thank them enough. To my husband, my first alpha reader, thank you for helping to bounce story ideas off of and helping me identify my 'that' and 'all' problems— and all the problems that have yet to be identified!

To my Yas, I cannot express how much your support and cheerleading helped to get me through the imposter syndrome moments. And a special thank you to the QueenYa for all of your help in 'fixing' my attempts to create a cover, logo, bookmark, etc. and advice on creating my small business! As always, the covers shine after being in your masterful hands!

To my Author Ever After community, thank you for lighting the fire under me and helping to walk me through the intimidating process of self-publishing.

Also by Jillian Beane

The Elemental Series

Elements: A Moment In Time *(prequel scene)*

Elements: A Battle Before *(prequel novella)*

Elements & Flame *(March 2024)*

Elements & the Fae *(Summer 2024)*

Elements & a Key *(Spring 2025)*

About Jillian

Jillian has been writing since high school. Finally published 25+ years later, she has had oodles of careers to keep her busy along the way....

Stay-at-home mom

Preschool Teaching Assistant

Licensed Journeyman Plumber

Secret Squirrel

Security for a Professional Baseball Team

Disability Adjudicator

Credit Card Fraud Investigator

Does she know what she wants to do when she grows up? Nah! Where's the surprise in that?!?!

Surrounded by the support of her loving husband, her two amazing and crazy kids and her family, she is adding AUTHOR to her ever-growing list of careers.

When she isn't writing, you can find her reading, watching movies, listening to music, or hanging out with her Yas at their favorite art studio getting into ALL the shenanigans. Whether creating with her words or her hands, Jillian finds joy in art of all forms, be it remodeling or building homes, crochet, painting on canvas or pottery, or simply sitting in front of the dreaded blinking cursor, preparing to go on an adventure with her imaginary friends.